THE LAST OF

Timothy Findley (1930–2002) is the author of ten novels, three collections of short stories, four plays, and two books of non-fiction. His first novel, *The Last of the Crazy People,* was published in 1967 and his second, *The Butterfly Plague,* was published in 1969. His novel *The Wars,* published in 1977, won the Governor General's Award and established him as one of Canada's leading writers. *Famous Last Words,* a best-selling novel of gripping international intrigue, was published in 1981. *Not Wanted on the Voyage* (1984) is the brilliant retelling of the story of Noah and his ark. *The Telling of Lies* (1989), an unconventional mystery set on the coast of Maine, won the Edgar Award. His later novels include *Headhunter* (1993), *The Piano Man's Daughter* (1995), *You Went Away* (1996), *Pilgrim* (1999), and *Spadework* (2001). His three story collections, *Dinner Along the Amazon* (1984), *Stones* (1988), and *Dust to Dust* (1997), were published to immediate critical acclaim, *Stones* winning the Trillium Books Award. His plays include *Can You See Me Yet?,* *The Stillborn Lover,* and *Elizabeth Rex,* which was a critical triumph at the 2000 season of the Stratford Festival and won the Governor General's Award. His non-fiction books include *Inside Memory: Pages from a Writer's Workshop* (1991) and *From Stone Orchard: A Collection of Memories* (1998).

One of Canada's most beloved writers, Findley was named an Officer of the Order of Canada in 1986, and was made a Chevalier dans l'Ordre des Arts et des Lettres by the French government in 1996. Born in Toronto, Findley lived for many years on a farm near Cannington, Ontario, with his lifetime companion, the screenwriter Bill Whitehead. Findley and Whitehead later moved to Stratford, Ontario, and divided their time between there and the south of France.

TiMOTHY FiNDLEY
THE LAST OF THE CRAZY PEOPLE

PENGUIN
CANADA

PENGUIN CANADA

Published by the Penguin Group

Penguin Books, a division of Pearson Canada, 10 Alcorn Avenue, Toronto, Ontario,
Canada M4V 3B2

Penguin Books Ltd, 80 Strand, London WC2R 0RL, England

Penguin Putnam Inc., 375 Hudson Street, New York, New York 10014, U.S.A.

Penguin Books Australia Ltd, 250 Camberwell Road, Camberwell, Victoria 3124, Australia

Penguin Books India (P) Ltd, 11, Community Centre, Panchsheel Park,
New Delhi – 110 017, India

Penguin Books (NZ) Ltd, cnr Rosedale and Airborne Roads, Albany, Auckland 1310, New
Zealand

Penguin Books (South Africa) (Pty) Ltd, 24 Sturdee Avenue, Rosebank 2196, South Africa

Penguin Books Ltd, Registered Offices: 80 Strand, London WC2R 0RL, England

First published in Canada by General Publishing Co. Ltd., 1981
Published in Penguin Books, 1983
Published in this edition, 1996

7 9 10 8

*Publisher's note: This book is a work of fiction. Names, characters, places and incidents either
are the product of the author's imagination or are used fictitiously, and any resemblance to
actual persons living or dead, events, or locales is entirely coincidental.*

Manufactured in Canada

Canadian Cataloguing in Publication Data

Findley, Timothy, 1930–2002
The last of the crazy people

ISBN 0-14-024119-1 (Trade edition)

1. Title.

PS8511.I38L3 1979   C813'.54   C93-093422-9
PR9199.3.F55L3 1996

Visit Penguin Books' website at **www.penguin.ca**

For WILLIAM WHITEHEAD

Prologue

All night long, Hooker Winslow's eyes were open.

Around the room, the first shadows of morning began to lift themselves out of the corners and up from behind the chairs. The curtains—or something in the curtains—motioned and moved and waved. Hooker watched.

On his bed Little Bones, his cat, lay sprawled and warm, enduring a dream. Her legs twitched. Hooker watched the dream very carefully. It was like his own, the one that always ended with a wakened stare.

It was hot. And yet it was September. It should not be hot, but it was—just as it had always been, it seemed, since spring.

When had it rained?

It hadn't. It was already September fifteenth, and it hadn't rained all summer. Not once. Everyone complained. It was so dry they could not sweat—or, if they could, it seemed to make them ill. It was so dry that the leaves has withered and the grass had turned yellow. Autumn hardly needed to come, everything was so completely desiccated. It was the sort of absolute drought that could even enter a person's mind.

1

Faraway, in the other rooms of the house, the family slept amid arid sheets, sweatless and exhausted—a mother...a father...an aunt. Also the maid. Somewhere, too, the other cats that Hooker harbored slept in circles against whatever cement or stone coldness they could find.

Somebody gave a cough. Hooker started.

They must not wake up. Not yet.

His horde of silences fell back into place. No one awoke.

Hooker lay flat and pulled aside the sheet.

There was his body, loosely covered in an undershirt and shorts. He was small for his eleven years, but his feet seemed to be far away. He could barely see them in the gray light He waved them back and forth. Yes. They were all right. But the other parts of him apparently were asleep. He turned his hands. Staring at the edge of the mattress, he began to hum the tune of "Frankie and Johnnie."

And the noises began.

At first there was just the remembered sound of his brother's voice, which swayed around lightly in his mind like audible smoke. Indistinctly and wordlessly it seemed to surround the sound of Hooker's name, but it was not quite prepared to say it aloud. The fragments, in slow motion, bounced back and forth, tantalizing him with their uncertainty.

One day...one night...one evening...Gilbert had talked for such a long time, in such a monotone, that Hooker was not certain that his brother was not still talking, somewhere, perhaps in his own room or in the library or out by the stable. Hooker could wait

The back-porch door whined open all at once and clappered shut. The air filled up with birds.

Two of the cats came outside into the yard. They slept under an old sofa on the screened-in back porch, out beyond the kitchen, where a lot of junky, unused furniture was kept for summer napping.

Now they languished a moment below the wooden, single step and stretched their forepaws in the dust, scudding up brown marks into the air. They advanced into the grassy part of the yard, making chirrupy noises, very like birds or mice. They paid no apparent attention to each other, although they moved in perfect unison toward the stable.

Hooker threw a piece of dead wood at them. They looked surprised. They started back onto their hind legs and then eased forward gingerly. They obviously wanted to see what had landed beside them, but Hooker threw again, and they both ran away, scuttling like rabbits deep under the shelter of the back porch. They did not reappear.

He settled down again to wait.

The dew dried up.

Hooker slinked his eyes and stared. The birds appeared from everywhere and stood in pointed attitudes, looking at the hosts of prey around them.

A wordless procession of syllables—strident, harsh and absolute—clattered across the innards of his mind, like smooth round stones rolling inside a wooden box.

Through a long dark hallway, a few gray faces approached in a shuffle up toward his eyes. Their mouths moved. They drifted....

Hooker drifted, became dizzy, and wanted to vomit.

He rose to his knees. The sickness mounted, full of noise and ache and fear. He felt himself urinating inside his trousers. He drifted further—and stopped.

Gradually his senses returned to him, and he lay down in the straw—wet, but hardly aware of it.

The birds motioned about in a dance on the lawn. There seemed to be a lot of singing.

Slowly, Hooker's eyes focused on the window of his mother's room. Little, pale, sand-colored curtains blew out from within, stretching at him like beckoning hands. They were made of chiffon so light that they looked like crushed smoke.

Across the yard it remained quiet, and there was a moment that was utterly static, before another breeze arose and stirred the curtains. Hopelessly Hooker saw the sky.

There was heaven.

It was so clean. It looked washed over with bleach and faded—too long in the sun. It looked, in fact, ready for something new to happen to it, like a change of moons.

Below him, in the barn, there came a noise.

He reached for the box. Would it begin...?

But it was only Little Bones.

She circled below him on the cement, slashing with her tail. She made a lowing, catty noise of anger. When she saw Hooker, she scrambled up the post.

He touched her on the head, and they lay back out of sight.

She watched him with a pale bronze stare. For a moment, too, Hooker looked back at her. She had funny, odd, blown-up eyes that he had seen somewhere before. Little, nervously flicking spheres of innocence and age in scattered colors. They were deadly, vibrant, yet clouded—gathered. They were explosions—like his. Just like his own eyes. There.

Now, the boy and the cat waited and were still.

Chapter One

On the last day of school, in June, Hooker had looked at the crowded, busy schoolyard, and he had sighed with relief. He could never be made to come back.

In the fall, when he was to be twelve, his father was sending him to boarding school, and consequently he would not have to see again these children who lived in the town with him and who knew about his mother. He could forget them. And he did.

Now, he smiled through the iron railings at the last bright sight of it all and at the very last sound of it, too. The boys at Markham College, and the teachers there, were to be strangers to him—and he would never tell them anything. Never.

He was free.

He walked home slowly under elm umbrellas far above his head—pale green against the sky. His books bounced against his back, from side to side, and the weight of them made him feel older and strong. He mussed his shoes in a puddle of water. He gazed imperiously at the houses, knowing that soon he would be a stranger to them as well—that no one, anywhere in town, would know him.

It was two o'clock.

Hooker took up a stick and drew it after him along the fences as he walked. It clattered softly, rhythmically, against the boards.

He thought about his mother and their troubles.

Some of the happenings which made up the trouble took place behind his back. For instance, quite often he heard arguing, and very often he knew that someone, somewhere, was crying. And many times, too, he was taken for sudden walks by Iris who was the Negro maid. Sometimes he would hear such phrases as "I can't, oh, I can't...." and "Don't make me do that...." from faraway upstairs. For two months in the autumn he had barely seen his mother, and then, from December to February, he did not see her at all. But he heard her. Weeping...crying...complaining...making noises and saying words that he did not understand. In March she went to the hospital, and in April she came home. She had given birth to a dead child.

All through the house they closed doors and drew shades.

His father chose a new room, one that had once been a den upstairs, and he moved in there, alone. Aunt Rosetta took over, completely, all the household duties. Iris took training once a week downtown with the St. John's Ambulance nurses—and his brother Gilbert stood for even longer periods, now, around doorways, and at the foot of the stairs, with his glass in his hand, looking odd and fat and useless.

As people, they solidified—it was true—and they became the absolutes of all the little things that once they had only partly been. They "froze," as Hooker said. They got dead quiet and looked at each other all the time, talking with their eyes above his head. All except Iris Browne, the maid, who would listen to him and talk to him in the kitchen.

Hooker knew, for himself, that he had looked forward to seeing a baby and that the baby had never come home. "It happened dead...." someone had said, and he was sorry because in his mind he had already seen its face. He called it Patrick, because they had said it would be called Patrick, after Aunt Rosetta's and his father's dead brother. It became a minor superstition for a while that people named Patrick died very oddly, and for two weeks at school, he had waited for Patrick Farley to fall dead in the yard or to clutch himself in the gym class and die on the spot. Eventually, however, he gave up waiting for that and concentrated all his fear and apprehension on his mother.

She came home. That was April. He saw her once on the day of her arrival.

"Don't stand right there, honey, in the doorway," said Iris. "Stand back outa the way."

Beyond the front door, on the walk, his mother, dressed in a pale, furry coat that perfectly matched the pallor of her skin, was being supported step by step— Gil on one side, Rosetta on the other—toward the great front of the house and the dark of the hall. Her color frightened him. She did not look real. She was dead. Perhaps she really was.

But she did not curve over, as he had thought she might. Instead she stood erect to let the neighbors see her, and she spoke.

"Yes. I lost it," she said out loud.

Hooker's eyebrows met.

"Who's she talking to?" he said to Iris.

"I don't know," said Iris. "I don't know, honey. Stand back."

Jessica Winslow set up a vulgar, vicious tirade, straining at her supporters' hands, which were trying to halt her progress, and finally standing free to one side.

Hooker ran into the living room. He looked from the windows there, across the muddy lawn.

"It's Mrs. Gaylor," he said. "She's watching at the hedge with a bag in her hand."

"Come back here," said Iris.

"But Mother's shouting at her. Why is she shouting like that at only Mrs. Gaylor?"

"'Cause Mrs. Gaylor's rude and stares," said Iris, folding her yellow-brown arm across Hooker's shoulder to hold him still. "Stand up."

The parade of noise and pain approached.

It mounted the steps.

"I'd like to know where the hell your father is," said Iris quietly.

Hooker looked at her face. He noticed at once the harsh expression of concern that was there and the pinched look that must very soon mean tears.

He stared away toward the trio on the step. They loomed up into the doorway.

For a moment he wished they would not come in.

The house whispered around his head. A thought—something about an old fear of being left alone—caught at him inside and tugged at him, like seaweed pulling free from a rock in the tide.

The doors remained open.

Around the figures on the threshold, the sun drew a line of light. Momentarily, they floated in space.

"Hold her, Gilbert," said Rosetta.

A small figure detached itself, and leaving its aura behind, it flitted to the hall stand and removed gloves and hat, and, amazingly, threw its coat in a heap on the floor. Then it rejoined the others.

"You're going to go upstairs," it said, in Aunt Rosetta's sharpened voice. "Now."

"Yes, Rosetta."

That was different. It was not the same at all as the voice that had spoken on the walk outside. Now it was hollow and tired, almost recognizable.

"Gilbert will help you."

"Yes."

Gilbert said, "Yes, Mother. Come along. I will help you."

The two figures, now departed from the sunlight, passed into the shadows. They came to the foot of the stairs.

"Jessica?"

"Yes? What is it, Rosetta?"

"Be sure to take the stairs one at a time, dear."

Hooker's mother turned. She smiled.

"My dear Rose," she said to his aunt, "for heaven's sake, is there any other way?"

Rosetta attempted, but failed, to smile.

Gilbert with his mother began to climb.

Hooker, watching—never not watching for a second—moved instinctively against Iris' arm, which held him violently fast.

"No," said Iris in a whisper. "Stay put. She doesn't want you to see her now."

He fell back and accepted the support of her dried-up breasts, which broke aside from each other to let in his head very gently. She folded up one hand against his brow and held him at the waist with the other.

"It wasn't fair," said Jessie to Gilbert on the stairs. "The way they held me and tore at me." Hooker strained to hear her. "...all the time they slapped him and he was dead, I prayed, you know.... I had a dream about these stairs, Gillie, and the knives in the kitchen, too.... I had dreams about pillows and bath-tubs and toilets. Since the day he was born, every single time they let me go to sleep I had those dreams...."

The stick bing-banged along behind him, and he shifted the school bag, and he wondered if, today, he would see his mother. Probably not. She stayed in her room so often, in her bed or by the window in a chair, and not even the difference of the last day of school would bring her beyond her door to look at him or to speak his name. He hadn't heard her speak it for months.

When he got home, he thought, he would not even ask for her. He would talk, instead, to Iris in the kitchen. He would flash his report card at her, and she'd be proud of him. She'd probably laugh, as she usually did, and say to him, "So the straight-A kid has done it again!"

"So you done it, eh? A straight-A card. That calls for coffee. Have some?"

Iris laid the card between them in its envelope and poured out coffee into two mugs.

"Congratulations."

"Thank you," said Hooker.

They made a toast in silence and drank.

"So now you're ready to go to Markham College, huh?" she said. "Eh?"

"I guess so," said Hooker. "I hope so."

"I'll miss you," said Iris.

Hooker said, "Not till October."

"No. That's true. We have the summer. And what're you going to do?"

"Oh...go in the field. I got the graves to take care of."

"Hah! You and them birds."

"Well...someone has to do it."

She smiled. "I suppose so."

It was pleasant in the kitchen. Even cool.

Iris regarded her long, thin, yellowy arms. She smiled, and breathed silently, glad to be alive. She was nearing fifty now, which made her proud. She had never expected to live so long. Her mother had died of tuberculosis when she was still in her twenties. Her father had died of pneumonia at the age of thirty-nine. Her brother Walter had died at nineteen—another tubercular—and her older sister Hettie had died of a ruptured appendix when she was twenty-two and about to be married. Sometimes, in the quiet of her room, Iris counted over her dead: Mama, Papa, Walter, Hettie, three aunts, two uncles, and innumerable cousins. There had also been five other brothers and sisters who had not reached more than their first year.

There was a joke, at home, that when you were born, a disease was reserved for you and consequently a death. Her mother believed in a graceful acceptance of her color. But she died. Iris' father believed only in the curse of his color. He lived longer. But not much. It was poverty really that killed them both—and all the others. Iris' father forbade his children to be servants or to accept employment on the trains. Iris disobeyed him and survived. She was not too proud to work.

Ultimately, through the early foresight of Rosetta, who had a built-in knack for choosing suitable servants, Iris had come to be part of the Winslow household—but that was so long ago that no one ever tried to count the years. It had been long before the marriage of Nicholas and Jessie, and it had even been sometime before the end of that fabled lifetime which encompassed the semimythical figure of Grandfather Winslow.

The telephone rang.

Iris rose and crossed the floor. The telephone was attached to the wall near the dining room door.

"Winslow residence, Miss Iris Browne speaking. Yes?"

Hooker watched and listened.

"I told you, Harry," said Iris, "put 'em on the porch an' if I hafto, I'll leave a check in my own name." She waited. "That's right—separate bills, just like usual. All right, Harry. 'Bye now. Good-bye."

She hung up and crossed back.

"More coffee?" she asked.

"Nnnnn...yes."

"You always go to fool me," Iris laughed. "No... no...no...yes!"

15

She poured the coffee, black, into his mug and sat down.

"Your Aunt Rose'd kill me if she saw you drinkin' that…"

She lighted a cigarette.

"…or me doin' this. God help us if she walks in, eh, Hook?"

She sang quietly:

"Oh, bring on your rubber-tired hearses,
Oh, bring on your rubber-tired hacks.
They're takin' your man to the graveyard,
An' they ain't goin' to bring him back…."

She looked out the window, smiling.

Hooker looked over at her, aware of the yellow-brown color of her skin, this afternoon, against the white of her uniform. She was tired. Her hair, which she kept fairly short, frizzed out around her ears and was gray in places. She had a crackly, papery voice. As long as Hooker could remember, Iris had been there in the house. She'd been there as long as Gilbert, his brother, could remember, too—and Gilbert was over twenty years old now.

"Gilbert is to come 'n clean potatoes for me—four o'clock."

Hooker jumped. Their thoughts had met exactly, which always amazed him.

Many afternoons Gilbert did work for Iris to "sort of make himself handy." Tall and tired, he would stand at the sink, wear an apron, and tell Iris about the world and its troubles. About his theories and his

16

plans and his cures. And about history. As he stood there, he would peel off generous ribbons of potato jacket, brown, wet, and sandy, into a colander under the tap.

"What time is it now?" Hooker said, hoping to be told that he could take up his mother's tea tray.

"I don't know. Whenja leave school?"

"Two. We got out early."

"Then you ought to know better'n me."

Iris walked over to the sink, doused her cigarette under the tap, and threw it into the garbage pail.

The subject of his mother's tea tray rested in both their minds; there was just a momentary pause before Hooker spoke again.

"Why do you call yourself *Miss* Iris Browne?" he asked.

"It's my name, Hook."

"Your name's Iris. Harry Jarman would know who it was if you just said Iris. Why do you always go an' say *Miss* Iris Browne. Nobody knows who that is."

"What do you call yourself?" said Iris.

"Hook."

"I see."

She maneuvered things on the table top and found the report card in its envelope.

"See that?"

She held it up.

Hooker nodded.

"Seems to say something about Hooker Winslow, but there's nobody called plain Hook on this paper here."

She tossed it down.

"But on the *phone*," said Hooker, edging her further into argument, "you sound like yourself. Who else could it be?"

"It could be Iris Merton. Could be Iris Bailey. Could be Iris anybody, far as that crazy, lazy German boy knows."

"Not with your voice."

"Now what do you mean by that?"

"You speak Negro."

There.

Unavoidably Iris paused.

"I suppose I do," she said. But she wore a smile.

"An' yet you always say *Miss* Iris Browne."

She flared, "I got every right to my name. An' as for bein' a colored person—have you considered, Mister Hooker, how many other colored persons live in this town here? Lots," she said. "Lots of them and all of them with different names."

"And different colors," Hooker thought.

"There's lots of us here, and I intend to make it clear which one of us it is."

"Well…" said Hooker, "but it was the 'Miss' I really wanted to know about."

"Well, I'm not married, am I?"

"No."

"Then it's right to call myself Miss."

"Even to Harry Jarman?"

"Even to him. Don't your aunt always denounce herself as Miss Rosetta Winslow?"

"Yes."

"Well then…" Her hands flew up in exasperation. "Honest to God!" she said.

Hooker fell still.

She was somehow, unaccountably, angry. It confused him. He had only meant to make her argue with him.

"Why're you mad?" he said.

"I'm just mad 'cause your head's so damned big and innocent. Next time you think something about Miss Browne and not Miss Browne, you ask yourself a few questions instead of gettin' it wrong like half a brain would tell you is wrong."

"What's the matter?"

"You. You got a straight-A card, yet you're all buggered up, an' you're not even twelve years old."

Hooker recognized the forbidden word but sat very still.

"Oh, I know where you get it from. You get it from that Gilbert. Sometimes I could take him and hit him so hard he'd split down the middle, he makes me so mad. Where does he think we live—the States? We wasn't ever slaves, you know!"

"He says it's his rheumatic fever makes him say things like that."

"Ho! Rheumatic fever. Hah! Rheumatism is no cause to have such loud opinions," Iris said.

"I just mean he says it makes him lie there and think things."

"Stories!"

"It isn't stories. He says so himself."

"Like he probably says to you I can't be Miss Iris Browne? Is that right? Just 'cause I'm Negro? It was him started all that, wasn't it, now?"

Hooker did not reply.

Iris blew her nose.

"Anyway," she said, standing straighter and tucking her handkerchief into the sleeve of her uniform, "it's nothing for us to make a fight out of. Not now." She smiled and changed the subject. "When your father comes home, you ought to take in the card right away. He's gonna be proud of you, hon."

Hooker thought, "Not if I'm all buggered up." He blushed.

"I'll take it in later," he said.

The door swung open. It was Gilbert.

"Speak of the devil an' you get him," said Iris. "Sure as God."

Hooker looked at her, but she walked away toward the refrigerator. He thought that her elbows looked old.

"Oh?" said Gilbert.

He wore gray flannel trousers, a blue-and-white striped shirt, a tie, polished shoes—and his mouth hung open.

"You back from school, eh?"

"Yes," said Hooker.

"What's it like out?"

"Hot."

"I heard yelling. Did you actually pass or something?"

"Yes," said Hooker. "I passed." He waited, but nothing further was forthcoming.

"He got straight A's," said Iris quietly.

Gilbert said, "Oh...good."

After another moment, he said, "I guess that means a bicycle from Nick, eh?"

"Yes," said Hooker. "I s'pose so."

"My first major defeat!" said Gilbert. "No blue bicycle."

They laughed. Gilbert had wanted his bike to be blue. But he'd failed two subjects that year.

Now Hooker watched him with great care.

Gilbert got his apron from a drawer and wrapped it around his middle. He looped the top part of it over his neck. It had a frill. He stood there, tall and big, his hair receding, his eyes small and blue, his second chin a little wet with perspiration. Iris did up the apron strings behind his back, and he walked bleakly to the sink.

"There," she said.

"Thanks," said Gilbert. "So," he began the afternoon's conversation, "school's out, eh?"

"Yes," Hooker repeated.

"What're you going to do this summer then?"

"I don't know," said Hooker. "I have the field to look after. And the stable to do, I guess."

"Why don't you build a house out there right in the damn field. A house for your damn cats. Then when they kill something, you don't have to carry it so far to bury it. You just scratch a hole and throw it in."

"I don't mind," said Hook. "It's a pretty walk."

"With that wagon," said Gilbert.

Iris opened a bottle of beer and poured most of it into a glass. She set the glass on the tile by the sink.

"There," she said.

"Thanks," said Gilbert.

"I don't mind," said Hooker. "I've done it so often now, there's a path."

"How many birds have you buried? So far?" asked Gilbert, winking at Iris.

"I don't know. Twenty. I guess—I don't know. And a lot of mice."

Iris got out a large, dusty white bag of potatoes. She got out a paring knife. She got out the colander.

"There," she said.

"They kill very quick," said Hook. "In fact, I've never actually seen it yet. They always come and bring it to me afterward, but it's very quick, and there's never any noise at all." He thought about it. "The only thing is the bird usually has no eyes. Just its neck is broken. No missing feathers, no blood. Nothing. Then I get a box and my spoon, and take it off to the field."

Gilbert watched this recitation and then said, "You'll get sick of it. You will. And then there'll be dead birds all over the lawn. It's a wonder Rosetta lets you even keep those bloody things near the house— four cats!"

"But you don't mind them."

"They're vicious. I'd rather have a dog."

"But a dog makes noise."

"At least it's human," said Gilbert.

He finished rolling up his sleeves.

Iris silently approached from one side and turned on the cold-water tap.

"Cats are human, too," said Hooker. "Father doesn't mind them."

"Except he's allergic. Or Rosetta says he is."

"That's not the same thing, really."

They all paused.

Then Gilbert drank from the glass, put it down, and

wet his hands.

He looked at Iris.

She ran a little hot water, adjusting the tap perfectly.

She walked away.

"Thanks," said Gilbert.

He picked up the knife and started.

"So school is out, eh?" he said.

"Yes." Hooker sighed.

"What will you *do* all summer?"

"We could play croquet," said Hooker. They used to.

"You need to practice," said Gilbert. He judged the first potato with an expert stare and gouged out a few eyes. His knife squeaked.

"But you'll never practice with me."

"I don't need to," said Gilbert. Then he relented. "I'll play you maybe tomorrow."

"I'd rather play tonight."

Iris said, "I'll play. One game. After supper."

She said it with no animation at all, almost automatically.

"I'll get it set up, then," said Hooker. "Right now and be ready."

"Good, honey. Do that."

He left the kitchen and went off toward the side yard. As he went, he heard Gilbert starting off, this time truly in earnest.

"Now, Iris," he said, "I'm reading *Lee's Lieutenants*. And you know what? I've been thinking. If the South—"

Hooker heard Iris sigh.

He let the screen door close over quickly, and he took a first deep breath of free spring air.

"The South of *what*?" said Iris with practiced stupidity. And something else that Hooker could not quite put his finger on. A practiced something else.

It was always the same, every day, now, in the closed-up house. Two people talking, and the rest all silent.

Chapter Two

A little later that same afternoon, Rosetta Winslow stood in the hallway and looked around her with a delicate scrutiny.

She wore a pair of yellow-cotton workman's gloves, and an old, gray dusting rag rested over the inside of her elbow, next to her smock. She reached out and ran a gloved finger along the edge of the banister. It was perfectly clean.

Rosetta's face was round and small. It rarely smiled. Years ago she had suffered a stroke which had not only left one arm less useful to her than the other, but which had caught one whole side of her face forever in a youthful mask. Of course, she had always been pretty, but now the prettiness was thin and joyless— but unbreakable, like certain kinds of glass.

She listened, turning her head at an angle to the upper part of the house, but there was no sound there. Quite far away, she could hear Hooker pounding croquet hoops into the turf of the side yard.

"That's right," she said to herself. "School's over. Damn."

The thought made her move.

She went across the hall, from below the stairs, to

the long green velvet drapes that closed off the living room. She pulled them aside, their brass rings chinking in the quiet like dice, and then whooshed them quickly closed behind her.

The living room was cool, long, narrow, and expensive. It smelled of two kinds of wax and ended, faraway, in two sets of tall, open French doors, screened against the invasion of summer insects.

"It really is a most lovely room," Rosetta told herself. "Isn't it?"

Her gloved hands carefully inspected the surfaces of polished tables, lifted little glass things and replaced them, pulled her along beside the mantel, and on, past a row of books by a radio, toward the doors. She stood quiet and looked outside.

Lawn, close-cropped and green, spread itself before her, looking misty through the screens. To the north, to her right, she could see Hooker. Dressed for school as he was, he looked ludicrously neat for someone doing something manual. She bit back her inclination to speak to him about his good trousers. There would be no time now to start anything. Hooker's father would arrive soon, and the room had to be ready for him. She regarded the watch which hung loosely around her wrist. It was four forty-two. Yes, in just a few moments, her brother Nicholas would come through the door.

She went slowly back toward the hallway. The ash trays were empty, the coasters were set out. A rug waited for his shoes. The doors were pulled open. There were a few flowers in small Chinese vases, the fire screen had been polished, the evening paper from Toronto…cigarettes and matches…

Rosetta glanced up.

She was thinking about cobwebs. She'd been in with a duster on a stick—oh, when? yesterday? today? a few days ago? When? Ah, well.

She saw the little angels, plaster cast in the molding They were sweet, she thought, and very right in the old room. The ceiling was high and painted a distant, off-white shade, which gave it the added distinction of looking "period."

"God knows what the angels and cherubs and things are doing," she thought, "but they're pretty. And they're sweet. Yes. Sweet and pretty. Father used to laugh when he saw them."

The angels and cherubs, in fact, were supposed to be dancing. They carried, in fat little hands, huge garlands of flowers bound in ribbon. They strung them, laughing, floating, and running, in loops around the room, and the loops formed the continuity of the design as it went about the four walls. At each corner there were linked arabesques of plaster, which stood in bolder relief. The angels wore dresses, and the cherubs, fat and bumpy, flew about wingless and naked. There seemed to be two boy cherubs for every girl cherub. No one knew why. Some of them had ridiculously fat behinds, and they reminded Rosetta of the days when she had bathed Hooker, and even Gilbert, years ago in the little tub made of canvas that had stood on a table in the nursery upstairs.

"When?" she thought. "When—when was that?"

There was not a cobweb in sight. Only the plaster-gossamer dresses of the angels and the loop-loop-looping garlands of off-white flowers and ribbons.

Rosetta marched into the hall, drawing back one curtain as she went.

She plopped her rolled-up yellow gloves and her rag duster into the drawer in the hall table. Facing the mirror above it, she tightened the slim gray knot of her hair under its coarse black net.

"Soon," she thought, "even Hooker will be taller than I am. Oh, well."

She turned.

From beyond the door at the top of the stairs, she heard the intimation of a noise.

Was it Jess?

The free side of her face aped the other. A little blood drained away from the shallow pockets beneath her pale, blue eyes. She shut the drawer with a slow, precise bang.

She stepped forward to the foot of the stairs, facing up squarely and—it was odd—almost bravely, while the suggestion of the noise came again.

Rosetta rose up the stairway in impossible silence.

She got to the door. If she had had wings, they might have hummed very gently to hold her still as she listened.

From beyond the door there came a worn, thin voice speaking in a monotone.

Then there was silence.

Rosetta could never make out the words.

She waited.

In a moment she heard the closing of a book, as pages fell into place through tense and nervous fingers. Then the book snapped shut and was put aside. A drawer was opened. That, too, was shut. A key flicked over and then jangled together with other keys on a chain. Then there was no further sound.

Satisfied, Rosetta maneuvered herself gently away and back down the stairs.

The front door opened.

Chapter Three

Nicholas came in.

Rosetta, on the stairs, did not speak, but a feeling happened—almost like speech. She looked at him. She was eight years older than her brother, and he was the only other living member of her family.

He stood quietly, just inside the width of the front door, on the foot mat.

A little true love, an old pride, lifted inside her.

"Father would have done that, too," she thought. "Stand there like that, dressed like that, in this heat."

She stepped in his direction.

He wore a pale-gray summer overcoat, a black hat, a dark gray suit, and black shoes which looked as though they had been polished by the fathom.

Her hands took his gloves, his hat, his (once her father's) malacca cane. She stepped silently to the table beneath the mirror and laid each item in its place. Then she went back. Nicholas turned at the touch of her fingers on his shoulders. She removed the overcoat and hung it in the cupboard, on a wide wooden hanger. It smelled of the distant city office—of ink, paper, and cigarettes. It reminded her of this same hallway years ago: that other man, gray-haired and tired, that other coat collar, with that same expensive, distant smell—her father, who had died and left her.

She turned back one last time. Nicholas was so handsome. His hair, now reaching beyond gray to white, and his fine, tired eyes—they appeared to be fighting back the remaining images of a bad day. He reached for his breast-pocket handkerchief and nervously wiped away a little saliva from his lips and moustache. He thumbed the handkerchief back into place.

Nicholas gazed around the hallway and admitted with a look that the door at the top of the stairs was still there.

Rosetta looked at her own fingernails and waited.

Nicholas coughed.

He coughed again, a small, irritating smoker's cough.

Rosetta waited while it passed.

At last he moved.

"What did you do with your day?" he asked in a low, cough-covered voice.

Rosetta, from long practice, did not reply.

What she had "done" gleamed and glistened all about them as they moved into the living room.

"How many years," she thought, "haven't I answered that question?"

They went on through the green-velvet drapes, Rosetta stopping short by the entrance, Nicholas moving on to the chair he always sat in. It faced the windows in the spring and summer; it faced the fireplace in the fall and winter. He sat down with his back to her.

"He always has his back to me," she thought. "Why?"

"How is Jess?" he asked, picking up the paper from its place on a nearby table.

"In her room," said Rosetta, as if that was the only right answer to his question.

"Still?"

"Yes."

Pause.

"Of course," she added. "Reading her old notebooks."

"I wish someone would—"

"Yes...but..."

Each of them prepared to go on—but neither did.

Instead, Nicholas opened the paper.

And Rosetta said, "I'll get your drink. Tea today or sherry?"

"Here," said Nicholas.

He dangled a single key on a chain over the back of the chair, without turning around. This meant sherry.

Rosetta went over and took it.

"Hooker passed," she said.

"Passed what?"

"His grades, Nick. This was the last day of school. It's holidays now. He got a very good card, but I'm not supposed to know yet. It's in the kitchen."

"I see."

Rosetta waited briefly and then left the room.

Nicholas sat with the open paper in front of him. He did not read. He could not, because he had not put on his glasses. He just sat there and coughed a little.

He heard Rosetta:

"Hooker!"

And he heard a more distant Hooker:

"Yes'm."

"Your father."

"Yes'm."

"Wash your hands," said Rosetta.

"Yes."

Nicholas sighed. He fingered his tie. He thought about the heat and the city. He tried not to think of his wife.

"Perhaps I'll take a bath," he thought. "Later I'll chip a few balls...have some iced tea...read something...go upstairs..."

Jess.

When he got to the top of the stairs, Nicholas paused. Staring at the closed door in front of him, he could not help thinking: "This is my room. Why shouldn't I go in there?" The thought trespassed in his mind, just as he wished that he could be strong enough to trespass beyond the door.

But he didn't.

He was standing there like that when Hooker came into the hallway below him. Nicholas did not hear his son, not even when he came part way up the stairs behind him.

Hooker, intent on the bathroom, where he would wash and make himself presentable for his father, did not notice Nicholas at first—and when he did, he almost spoke aloud. But he refrained. Instead, he stood still, halfway up the stairs, watching and listening.

Nicholas approached the door.

"Jessie?" His voice was soft and unrecognizable.

There was no reply.

"How are you, Jess?" Pause. "Dear?"

Hooker watched his father's back It looked tense, and it was pressing forward in such a way that it seemed to be trying to meet the breast bone in front of it. Nicholas got right to the door and stood up straight before it—not like someone listening or about to enter the room beyond, but like someone actually addressing the door, as though the door were the real recipient of his words.

"Have you rested today?"

There was still no answer.

"I wish you'd let me come in, Jess."

Now Hooker, too, began to hope for an answer. While Nicholas wanted the answer to reassure himself, Hooker wanted it so that his father would not make a fool of himself. But it was apparently as much a foregone conclusion that Jess would not reply as it was that neither would the door.

To save himself from the confusion of a confrontation, Hooker began to retreat. He tripped. He had made the mistake of retreating backward. He did not fall, but his heels struck against the banisters, and Nicholas slowly turned and stared at him.

"What are you doing there?"

"Going to the bathroom."

"On the stairs?" Nicholas made this reply from a particularly desiccated sense of humor—it had never been a lively one—and consequently his words came out with a kind of deadly calm that frightened Hooker.

"No, sir. I mean I was going upstairs to wash."

Really, Nicholas thought, the child has no sense of humor.

"Well, then, go on," he said. "You'll be late for supper."

"Yes."

Hooker continued on up and passed his father and disappeared into the bathroom. The door closed behind him.

Nicholas, before going on to the converted den where he slept and into which all his clothes had been moved, turned back to the bedroom door and placed his hand on the knob.

In a sense, his hope was that the door would be locked, but his conscious thought was that it would be open. Which it was.

He looked and then went in.

He felt like a child. His first thought was: If Rosetta catches me in here, she'll kill me. And then he looked at his wife.

There was a chair by the window, and Jessie sat there asleep in a blue robe.

Blue was a suitable color and always had been for Jess. It did the right things for her hair and for her eyes. But her hair, now, was tied with a sort of broad and ugly ribbon, and her eyes were closed.

He stared at her.

They had lived together for over twenty years. A war ago. A business career ago. A marriage ago. Three children ago. A life ago. Forever. He did not really know this woman asleep in the chair. Who was she? She was not the woman he had known and married—beautiful, sensitive, in some ways even fun, although

35

never beyond the point of propriety. She had worn clothes well, and wealth. She had led the proper life for the wife of a Winslow. Except that her parents had divorced; she had come to him out of the secrecy of a torn home. Her mother had gone "peculiar"—as her friends had said, trying to be kind—and she had died quite soon of boredom and confusion. Her father had remarried and disappeared. But Jessie had remained aloof from the emotions involved in all of this. Or apparently she had. In truth, it had eaten into her sense of security. Privately she had withdrawn from everyone she should normally have trusted. A year or two ago— was it then that the trouble had really begun?— Nicholas had found her in bed one morning, weeping uncontrollably. It was when she had first started not getting up for the boys' breakfast. He had said to her, "Jessie. Jess. What is the matter?" He was astonished because he had never seen her weep like this before. And she had looked at him suddenly—with a quick, unchallengeable hatred that was just not part of her character—and she had said, "You! God damn you. You and Gilbert and Hooker and my father—all of you. Failures. Bastards." She had begun to cry again—shaking but strangely quiet. Nicholas had been stunned. For he wasn't a failure. He had given her everything. But then she had looked at him again, and unaccountably, unreasonably—he always thought so afterwards, too— she gave him a sort of washed-out, stranger's stare, and she said, "My men. My men. All my men. Hopeless failures. Everyone of them. Useless. Hopeless. Failures."

Then she had remained in bed, where Iris for several days served her her meals and brought her books to read.

But that crisis, or whatever it had been, passed within a short time, and soon Jessie had come back into the family enthusiastically—her old self. On and off during the next year and a half she had had relapses and retired to her room for some—indeed for any—unaccountable reason. She simply withdrew. It was after this that, together, one late summer evening at the lake, they had decided to try for another child. They reasoned that Jessie needed to start caring again and that someone new would give her the chance to care in a new context—strongly, with a fresh beginning. But within weeks of knowing that she was pregnant, she began to have more frequent relapses, and finally the condition was permanent. Jessie didn't want a baby. The truth was, she didn't want to have to care. At least, that was the way Nicholas had reasoned. It was how he had finally given up.

It would soon be suppertime. Jessie would wake up and ring her little brass bell. Of course, she must not find him there. He could not face another screaming fit—or whatever it was you called whatever possessed her when she saw him. An hysterical reaction to reality. Someone had said: "Never manifest reality."

He stepped away.

Before he left her, he took a quick look around the room. There were her books—mostly religious books, it seemed—Thomas a Kempis, St. Augustine, The Life of St. Theresa of Avila. And there, too, were her own notebooks and the box she kept them in. The box was unlocked, now, and open. She had been reading over her old thoughts.

Nicholas thought: "How futile." To put down all that stuff—bits of poetry...maxims...religious verses...and imagined guidance from God—just so you could tell yourself, later on, that once...once...once...once... once, some long, long time ago, you'd had a chance to reason with and to appreciate and to savor the mind of mankind. And to take part. "You put it in a book," Nicholas thought, closing his wife's door, "and then you never have to do it."

After supper, as they did some very few nights, Nicholas and Rosetta watched the news on television and then one of the westerns. But the TV did not, as a rule, get turned on at all. Jessie complained of its noise. So, in the evenings, Gilbert, Hooker, and Iris gathered together on the back porch and sat on the old sofa or on the wicker chairs, talking and drinking Pepsi. Gilbert would drink beer. They played word games (Gilbert's choice) or card games (Hooker's choice), or they just sat (Iris' choice). However, on some evenings, such as this one, Iris sang. She had started the singing when Gilbert was a child, and it had gone on into the years that followed. The favorite song was "Frankie and Johnnie," sung off key.

> "Frankie and Johnnie were lovers!
> Oh, lordy, how they could love!
> They swore to be true to each other,
> Just as true as the stars above—
> He was her man,
> But he done her wrong."

"Go on," said Hooker.

"No. It's too loud and too long. Your mama would come down here and shoot us," Iris laughed. "Like she says she will about the TV."

"Anyway, it'd get her to come down."

"She'll come down, someday."

"The day you sing on key, she'll come down out of sheer amazement," said Gilbert.

They laughed.

Then Hooker said, "Tell about the song, Iris."

"I've told it before."

"And before..." Gilbert said. "And before and before and before."

They all knew this was true.

"But tell it again," said Hooker.

Gilbert winked at Iris. "At least," he said, "he doesn't ask for the three little pigs or any of that crap."

"I never did," said Hooker.

"Well, go ahead and tell him, Iris," said Gilbert. "Tell about Frankie and Johnnie. There's nothing like a good murder story."

Iris spread her leathery fingers before her on her uniformed legs and gave them a critical look. Then she said softly, not looking at either Gilbert or Hooker, "Ah, but it's not, you see. It's not the story of a murder."

"What is it, then?"

"It's a love story."

"A love story!"

"Yes."

"Phooey!"

Hooker blinked in anticipation.

Gilbert drank his beer from the bottle.

Iris lighted a cigarette.

She spoke slowly. "This story of Frankie and Johnnie, it's about the town I come from, you know. Carter's Bridge. Down near Niag'ra, there. This was one of those towns, all colored, from the days of the underground railway: All we colored people set up freedom towns, you know, when we escaped the slavery down south."

"You were never a slave, you said."

"I wasn't. Nor was my dad. Or, I guess, his dad. But the first people in Carter's Bridge were escaped slaves and truly black. Not yellow like me."

"Okay. Go on."

"Frankie and Johnnie took place in and around Carter's Bridge in 1921. It's about a colored woman and a no-good mulatto man."

Gilbert laughed his disbelief.

"It's about two spades in St. Louis, Missouri," he said.

"Don't say 'spade' like that, Gilbert," said Iris. And then she added quietly, "An' don't say St. Louis, Missouri, neither. This story happens to be true."

Gilbert, smiling, stole and lighted one of her cigarettes. He knew exactly how to irritate her. You only had to contradict her.

Iris continued. "It's about this Negro and this mulatto who lived near Carter's Bridge. My mom told me this song before she died, so you shut up about spades and things. And about St. Louis, Missouri. If we people had lived right in *Toronto*, let alone Carter's Bridge, in 1921, it could even have happened there. So shut up."

"Very well," said Gilbert, affecting world-weary acceptance. He knew damn well it was really about two nigs in St. Louis and not about anybody in Ontario, but this probably didn't matter to Hooker, for whom the song was being sung, anyway. Iris, just because she was Negro and had been raised down there near Niag'ra, was always trying to instill in Hooker's mind that the Negro was a noble figure of tragedy. She illustrated this not only by reciting her own folklore but by lifting the folklore of the Indians, the Chinese, and the Jews. She even told the Bible stories that way: David was a Negro youth and Goliath was a white man, the one a resident of Carter's Bridge, the other of Toronto; Job lived in Africa; Abraham and Isaac came from Alabama or somewhere, and the ram they found and killed was a plantation animal; Hagar and Ishmael had wandered on a North American desert, etc. She did not reinterpret the New Testament. Only the Old. But of all the stories and all the songs, "Frankie and Johnnie" was the favorite, because it told about liquor and jealousy and guns and murder. Now, she said it was a love story! He'd heard everything. Nevertheless, he remained and liskned, drinking his beer while Iris explained it all to his young brother, who sat in the porch twilight, leaning across the sofa toward the story teller, enraptured by what he was told.

Hooker, Gilbert thought just before he began to listen himself to Iris, would believe anything. He'd believe it if you told him that the world was going to end.

"Frankie," said Iris, "was a colored girl. She was really called Frances Gaylord. She was clever. She traded in land, and, you see, later on she sold it to the white people. So Frankie had some money. She fell in love with this mulatto man—Jonathan White. And that was when the trouble began. Other folks—the Negroes and the whites—didn't like her fooling around, spending her money on a half-breed person who drank liquor and didn't work. But Frankie said, Johnnie is a good man. He loves me an' I love him, and if I want to buy him clothes and liquor and a Bulova wristwatch, that's my business and not yours. So she went on loving him, until one day she discovered that Johnnie had another woman stashed away in a hotel room somewhere. This hotel, let us say, was right in the heart of downtown Carter's Bridge. Frankie heard this from the bootlegger. So she went to this hotel, and there was Johnnie with a white girl. She was what you call a prostitute. He was drinking liquor, you see, and kissing this white girl, and he told Frankie to go away and leave him alone. Well, this made Frankie see red. She thought how she'd defended him in front of other people. She thought of the clothes she'd bought him, and she thought of the liquor from the bootlegger, and also, she thought of the Bulova wristwatch and how much she had loved him. Frankie had a Negro's pride. She also had a gun. And she took this gun and her pride downtown, and she went into that hotel in Carter's Bridge and up to Johnnie's room where she shot him dead. But before he died, Johnnie said to Frankie: Frankie, believe me, it was really you I loved. This white girl didn't mean nothing to me. I just had her for a few kisses. And Frankie said: Oh Johnnie, you was my man an' you did me wrong, but I forgive you.

And Johnnie said: Roll me over, Frankie—he was lying up against the wall, where he fell when she shot him, you see—and he said: Roll me over real careful, 'cause I hurt where you killed me and let me see you one last time. So Frankie rolled him over on his left side, very careful. And she kissed him good-bye, and he said: Frankie, I was your man. Believe me. I was. But I did do you wrong. I know you loved me so it's okay. And he died forgiving her that way."

"He didn't forgive her or any damn thing like it," said Gilbert.

"He forgave her. And the reason he forgave her was that Frankie loved him. When the judge and jury heard her story, they forgave her, too, and they said: Frankie, because you loved him so much you killed Johnnie White. We know he was your man, but there is no doubt about it—he did you wrong. You have killed him for love. And that's the end of the song."

Gilbert grunted general disapproval.

"Nobody kills someone they love," he said.

"Maybe not," said Iris. "But they will kill *because* of love. Perhaps they kill some people because they love them so bad that they can't stand to see them do wrong that way. Or because they can't stand the unhappiness anymore."

"What unhappiness?"

"The unhappiness of loving someone who does useless things—or who's bad."

They thought about it silently.

The twilight settled, and it became dark outside beyond the screens.

There was a long quiet.

Then Hooker said, "What's a prostitute?"

And Gilbert laughed.

"So much for love," he said.

But inside, where he hoarded so much, so many words for quoting, he was thinking:

> "Yet each man kills the thing he loves,
>   By each let this be heard,
>   Some do it with a bitter look,
>   Some with a flattering word,
>   The coward does it with a kiss,
>   The brave man with a sword!"

In the last dim light from the sky, he regarded his brother and Iris. Oscar Wilde was queer. Frankie was a spade. The world was made of strangeness, madness, and fear. And the weirdest people found each other in love.

He got up to get himself another bottle of beer.

Iris said, "Me too, I'm thirsty."

Hooker began to hum:

> "Frankie and Johnnie were lovers!
>   Oh, lordy, how they could love!
>   They swore to be true to each other,
>   Just as true as the stars above...."

For the last part, they all sang together.

Gilbert went into the kitchen.

Summer had begun.

Chapter Four

Over the winter and through the spring, Hooker had been on many walks with Iris. Each was precipitated by some occurrence beyond the closed door of his mother's room.

Hooker could recognize the exact moment of his departure. On these occasions, he would quietly take his own coat or windbreaker off the hook and lay it on the hall chair, and sit there patiently until Iris came to take him away.

The noises upstairs were always of a kind—crying... thumping...or plain argument. The first rush of feet would inevitably be Rosetta. She'd come out of her office in the back hall, get to the foot of the stairs, listen—and then call Iris.

Iris would come, drying her hands, from the kitchen, by which time Rosetta would already have mounted the stairs. Then they would go in, one after the other. Sometimes they had to telephone the doctor, and on these occasions the sounds from the bedroom would be most persistent and drawn out. Hooker would watch the carpet, and very often, he would pray, for his mother had taught him to rely on prayer in all instances of confusion. In the old days, she would have prayed with him.

But not anymore.

Then, in the hallway, where he was waiting, there would eventually be total silence. The door would open. Down would come Iris, talking back up the stairs.

"Yes, Miss Rose," she would say. "I gotcha, Miss Rose. Right away, Miss Rose. Oh, I'm sure he'll be delighted."

Always, it was assumed that Hooker was blind and deaf.

"Come on, then." And even Iris would pretend to believe it as she said it. "Today we'll go and see the zoo."

And Hooker would rise, with his coat already half on.

Iris, who was not only very thin but tall, took large and energetic steps. She was relentless, once she started, until the far corner had been reached and turned. Hooker had to skip and run just to keep pace with her. Then she would stop and open her old leather purse, from which she pulled cigarettes and gum.

"I'm going to smoke now," she would say, "and you may chew."

The gum package was inevitably new and unopened. Hooker never knew when she finished one and bought another. She undid the cellophane. In truth, the cigarettes and gum were delivered with the groceries by Harry Jarman, and it was these Iris paid for by personal check.

"Here," she said.

Hooker accepted the little individual piece of scented gum and solemnly began to chew, while Iris lighted up.

"Now we can walk slow," she said, breathing heavily of smoke.

They started away down the street in earnest, "walking slow." It was the important part of the journey. This was a quiet place to walk, and the houses, set far back behind their gardens, were blind people, calm and uncaring. There was never anyone about, except an occasional dog, asleep.

"Just look at that day," Iris said.

She gestured broadly at all that the day contained of sky, trees, weather, and snow, for on this occasion, it was winter.

"It is a good thing, whether you know it or not, just to be alive," she said, hugging her coat around her.

They walked on slowly, almost hanging back from the destination they moved to. Their breath showed. It was such a quiet street that it was easy, there, to make the world seem different and calm and ordinary.

"Is mother always going to take on?" said Hook. "And do things?"

"No," said Iris, lying.

"It seems she has for a long time," he said.

"It is…some time. But not to worry."

"Iris?"

"Yes?"

"When she didn't, that was when she came downstairs *all* the time?"

"That's right."

Hooker tried to remember it.

It seemed so long since his mother had been an

actual part of his family. Once she had been fun and happy, although she had always been a quiet person. He remembered the prayers they had said: "Gentle Jesus, meek and mild…" That was his mother, too, gentle and meek and mild.

"Iris?"

"Yes?"

"Tell about a baby coming."

"I told it."

"Then tell me again."

"Well, all right, but don't chew so damn loud. I can't think straight then, and it gets in the way of this story."

Hooker rolled his gum into a silent ball in one corner of his mouth.

"Where do I begin? Let me see now, you was a baby…."

"Yes," said Hooker, "I was a baby."

"An' you were such a grand baby that you made your mom swell up. With pride. See? Because she knew how terrific you was going to be."

"How did she know I was going to be terrific?"

Iris grunted.

"It comes inside your mind, I guess. I guess you know what your baby's going to be like. An insight. See?"

"You've never had one. How do you know?"

"I don't say I know—I just say I guess. Anyhow, your mom swelled up with pride. A doctor calls this pride the pregnancy."

Iris' eyes moved sideways for a glimpse of the face beside her. After a puff of smoke she continued.

"Now, when the pregnancy gets too powerful, and

the mother just can't bear anymore being proud about something she can't see, she busts wide open and falls down, like your mama, and all the people rush round her, and the doctor brings the baby so she can see it."

"How?"

"He *brings* it."

"How, though?"

"He brings it. Outa your mother."

"Why does it have to be out of my mother?"

"Why not?"

"Well, what about my father? Can't he swell up, too?" Iris swallowed her gum.

"No," she said.

"I beg your pardon?" said Hooker.

"I said *no!*"

They began to walk faster.

One day, Hooker said, "My father has hurt my mother."

Iris stopped short.

"How do you mean?" she said.

"That's how I was born," said Hooker "and it's how they got the new baby."

Iris started to walk again. She did not want to lend the weight of stillness to the conversation's present turn.

She said, as casually as she could, "How do you mean that 'hurt,' exactly?"

"He takes my mother, and he makes her do things."

"Now, honey! What do you mean?"

Hooker paused, afraid.

Iris smiled encouragingly. "Tell me," she said.

"Well…he hurts her into being pregnant."

Iris gave a sigh.

"Who was you talking this over with?" she asked. "Harry Jarman?" Her voice was quiet. "Gilbert? Not that brother of yours, now?"

"No, I just heard it," said Hook, who genuinely had just heard something in the lane, over the fences.

"Boys!" said Iris.

"I'm never going to hurt a mother," said Hooker.

"You don't blame nobody for what's happened to your mom, do you?"

"Then who hurt her? Someone said they poke them with things."

"Nobody hurt her."

"You don't just get sick from nothing."

"I didn't say 'nothing.' I said no*body*. Sure something made her tired—and sick, a little. But you're not to lay blame on people. One day you will understand how it happens."

One day…one day…one day…

"When?"

"When you're old enough."

She marched on. From the way her pace gathered momentum, he knew that she would not answer any more questions, so he quickened his steps to follow her.

On another day, more recently, Hooker paused at the third comer and said, "It isn't fair that I have to marry a woman."

Iris stopped.

"Dearest heaven!" She threw up her arms. "Now, what made you say that?"

By now, the early summer sky was a hot white lid above them, blue at the edges.

"It's on my mind all the time."

"Who says you got to, anyhow? There isn't any law about stuff like that. All people old enough have the choice, and without being old enough it's no marriage anyhow."

"Little girls four get married in India."

"HO!"

"It's right in a book at school, Iris."

"Then it's an awful old-fashioned book. Pay no attention."

After a second, Hooker said, "Mama shouldn't have been married at all."

"Listen, you are going to have to stop that. You shouldn't speak on things you don't know about."

"But I do know about it. Mama should not have been married to father. Then she wouldn't be sick."

"And how then, may I ask, just how do you know?"

"Gilbert says so."

They had come to the Harrises' driveway. The Harrises were old and owned a dog. A friend of Iris' worked there.

Now Iris squinted along the gravel driveway and took a pause before she answered. A worried expression hung down from her forehead over her eyes.

"Gilbert, eh?" she said. "Well."

Then she paused again.

"Why don't we go in and talk to my friend Alberta?"

No answer.

"We could drink lemonade," she said.

"No."

"I'll take you to the movies."

"No."

"Go to the city? Ride the new subway?"

"No."

She scrutinized the house with exaggerated peering gestures. Mrs. Harris appeared at the window and waved. Iris waved back.

Hooker started away. Iris watched him.

"Hook?"

He turned.

She shaded her eyes with her hand in a fist, and she looked to Hooker like an advertisement lady with a headache.

"Do you want to see the dog?"

He shook his head and started away again.

"Here...Hooker!"

He turned again.

"What?"

She caught up with him. Iris smiled in a way he had never seen. It was lonely and sad. She held out her hand.

"Gum," she said.

He looked at her. Then he took the package absently. He was trying to figure out the look on her face. She was still smiling.

"Gilbert talks a lot," she said. They started walking again.

"I know he does," said Hooker, "but sometimes he's right."

"Not always, I hope," she added to herself. "But sometimes."

Out loud she said, "Maybe we can go and see the dog some other time."

Chapter Five

One by one, the summer evenings came and went.

"I want to play croquet," said Hooker.

"Shhh quiet!" said Gilbert. He puffed on one of Iris' cigarettes.

"What?"

"Rosetta and Nick—they're talking about me."

"Where?"

"In the living room."

"How do you hear that far?"

"I have the biggest ear holes in creation," said Gilbert.

"An' the biggest mouth hole, too," thought Iris. "Well, don't listen," she said aloud. "That's terrible rude."

They were sitting by the porch at the back of the house.

Hooker stood up and drifted away, followed by his cats.

"Bloody things..." said Gilbert. "Look at their damn behinds! Look at them. And he actually brings them into the house!"

"Funnier still," said Iris, watching Gil as he lifted

another cigarette from her packet, lying open on the step, "is Miss Rose—that she don't really seem to mind them. Sure she yells scat, but I never seen her ever kick 'em out of the house."

"They probably have something in common," said Gilbert. "Just look at those behinds."

"I wanta play croquet," said Hooker, moping further off.

"Then play!" said Gilbert.

"Don't yell," said Iris.

Hooker disappeared down the side lawn, near the living-room doors.

"I could stand a beer," said Gil to Iris. "And then just sit here for a while."

Iris rose, snorted, and coughed her way all the way to the refrigerator. She came back, beer in hand, wiping her mouth with her wrist.

"Here," she said and sat down again. "Aren't you supposed to go out tonight?"

"Yes," said Gilbert. "Later. Not for another hour, at least."

They listened to Hooker knocking croquet balls around.

"Well, then," said Iris, "since you're gonna sit for a while, what're you gonna talk about?" She sat back and looked at the trees.

"I don't know," said Gilbert. "Why don't we just have a quiz?"

"A quiz?" said Iris. "Unh-unh. All you wanta do is show off."

"But I like quizzes," said Gilbert.

"Well, I don't," said Iris.

"All right. Never mind, then. We'll just sit."

So they sat, and they breathed up the evening air and waited for a new thought to come.

It didn't. It was quiet.

From the croquet lawn, Hooker heard parts of the conversation between his father and his aunt.

"I found him standing outside her door again today, with his hand on the doorknob."

"Oh?"

"He was drunk, I guess. He was leaning against it as though he might fall down."

"What'd you do?"

"I told him she was sleeping. He gave me a funny—awful—look. Sour—sort of bitter. With his mouth down, you know, but smiling. He told me he wanted to speak to her. He said he wouldn't keep her long. I was afraid she'd open the door, because he kept knocking at it all the time we stood there. But I think she *was* asleep. Thank heaven. I wish he'd leave her alone. Hooker does. Hooker never even asks to see her now. He may be afraid, but at least he stays away from her."

Nicholas coughed once and then continued to cough in a lower key with a softer tone. Rosetta started to take all the pins from her hair. She did this only if she expected to be seated, talking, for some time. She would take them all out, adjust her hair net, and then carefully put them all back in, without the benefit of a mirror.

"He keeps trying to get at her all the time, Nick, as though he has something to say to her that he thinks will interest her. But he can't have anything to say.

How can he have? He can't. No one can. Not even you and I have anything to say—and Hooker hasn't, naturally, so how can Gilbert? And she barely ever mentions his name, except the other day she asked me how many girls he has. Phfff...tt! Girls! He's always going to parties, but you never hear him say he's met anyone. Or danced with anyone. I don't think he has a girl friend to his name."

She mouthed her pins.

Nicholas turned carefully in his chair.

"Sometimes," he said, "I wonder if he hasn't got the same sort of troubled mind she has. I remember..." He looked at the glass of iced tea beside him. He felt behind his ear; he smoked his cigarette; he ran his finger over his moustache; and then he carefully wiped his fingers, looking at them carefully, wiping them carefully, on his big, white, neatly folded, neatly refolded and thumbed handkerchief. And then he drank the iced tea and went on. "Every time," he said, now brushing a little bit of gray ash along the arm of the chair, "I lie awake thinking I must do something for him"—he maneuvered the ash to the end of the arm—"get him off some place, and will myself to be adamant, I remember"—he tilted his head forward, smoking and making little facial gestures of discomfort—"how when he was a child and two or three times he came into my bed"—Rosetta sat up very straight; Nicholas did not see her do it—"and lay with me"—straighter—"it was up at the cottage in the summer—at Lake Simcoe, at the cottage, and he was afraid of something, rain or something, and he lay stretched right out flat so I was aware of him from head to toe—

there would come this little shudder, this peculiar little shudder...."

Nicholas shook.

He drank. He smoked. And he said, "Then I remember"—tipping his head right over sideways—"lying there and thinking, This is not right This is not normal. He'd be asleep. You see. And there it was...."

Rosetta postured higher, turning, still very straight, to watch.

"You could feel it. Flick!" Nick's hand rose, open and twisting like someone screwing in a bulb. "Like a bubble. In his head. Then it would travel on down, right to his toes, and his foot would twitch, and then he'd go still. Still and"—Rosetta watched—"quiet." She blinked and went back to her pinning. Her back eased itself slowly and showed its age. "Then about a minute later, you'd feel it again."

He was concentrating with cruel attention on the exactness of the memory.

She said, "You mean, then, you're afraid of Gil, now—or about him?"

"I mean I don't know what to do. We've seen what happened to Jess. We've seen that happen. Right here. And it's going to happen again with Gil, right now. It's time to do something about him, especially because it can't be right to take the chance of his disturbing her—somehow. But I don't know what. I don't know what to do. I must—you must—we all must be afraid. He may be just like she is."

"But Jess will get better, dear. This is not permanent."

"For Christ's sake, Rose. Christ Almighty. Jesus."

He shook out his handkerchief.

She looked at him, mentally withdrew the lie, and then spoke.

"Well, I think," she said, "I think that if he's sick—like she is too, if you like—then I think we let them get sick."

"What?"

"Because of always being afraid. To *do* anything."

"You can't put a sick man out on the street. You can't put someone who's ill on a park bench, in a bread line. You can't."

"If you're afraid, you can't. No."

"He's not an ordinary person!"

Nick's eyes changed. He became just slightly redder than a man with sunburn.

Rosetta did not speak.

"You cannot put him there—now—and expect him to function like an ordinary person."

"You've never given him the chance to function like *any* kind of person."

They stared at one another.

"What?"

"Don't say 'what.' Don't look like that. I'm only telling you the truth, Nick."

He subsided in his chair. His legs, in front of him, looked childish and helpless. They lay, knees together and feet apart, like the legs of a paraplegic patient waiting for help. He pursed his lips.

"He's got to be something. *Be* something. Everybody is. I am someone. Everyone is something—someone. But he's not even a dead-proper bum!"

"That's your fault. Not his."

"Well, how do you kick him out, then? Tell me, for God's sake, how do you kick him out of here, his own home? Nobody ever kicked me out."

"Because you went out. What is not normal here at all is thinking—even having to think—about kicking him out. You shouldn't have to. Under circumstances—different ones, normal ones—you'd never even have to think that. He'd just go."

Rosetta watched Nick's face. He looked sick himself, she thought. His eyes, tired and full of fear, showed a readiness for this defeat that was not normal.

"It isn't normal," she thought "This simply is not a normal quota of trouble at all. This is different. It's like being marked for something. Like the Jews at Auschwitz."

"It's all been done before," said Nick. He spoke out of the depths of a long thought of his own. "Everything's been tried once and done twice. Before. He's had all kinds of jobs, and you know he just couldn't handle them. Not one of them. We'd swear he was going to work, for instance, and then we'd see him, by accident, in Toronto on the street, and I'd phone up wherever it was, and they'd say to me, 'Him? He hasn't been here for maybe a week.' A whole week! Then gradually he'd drift back home. Gradually he'd drift back to this house, and he'd apologize somehow, and he'd explain it. He always, always, always was able to explain it. He has a genius for explanations. That's what gets me. He has a marvelous, wonderful—*loaded* mind. I wonder sometimes, and sometimes I say to myself that the lad's got a wonderful mind. He has a mind that's incredible. I think—he's a latent poet. Do you know that? I think, here's someone who will probably write someday, or paint—or create something, and is just waiting now, simply waiting it out. Time. Waiting for the right time."

Rosetta watched Nick's face change as he began this dream—the old dream of Gilbert as someone brilliant he had hidden away in the family.

"Yes," he said, having just seen it all very clearly, "that's exactly what he is. A sick poet. And he really has been sick, too."

"No. Now don't talk like that! He's not sick. He's just a person who's been victimized by the bad habit of what you've allowed him to do—which is to lie still all the time instead of moving around."

"He's sick. He had rheumatic fever. That can be a dangerous thing, dangerous to live with all your life. An illness of the heart…"

"It is habit!" said Rosetta.

"Of the heart! Why, he's ill. That's what it really is. He is sick. And then there's that tic. Have you seen him drive the car? Doesn't react. Not properly. No reactions. Mark my words."

Nicholas sat in mime with a wide, impossible steering wheel before him, held in his open hands.

"His reactions are whole minutes behind my reactions. When he's driving, you can see it."

He threw away the wheel and stood up. He walked to the mantel to get more matches from a box there.

Rosetta watched.

"Habit," she said.

"All right, but you put a bad heart, a lack of control and coordination—put all those things, plus a tendency not to be able to turn up for appointments, which is quite a commonplace mania—or phobia—these days, put all those things together, and you've got someone who can't make his own way."

"He's a pathological…"

"What?"

"…bum."

Nick looked at his sister like an angry child.

"God damn it, Rosetta…"

Silence.

He looked at her, knowing what she thought.

In a moment, he said, "You don't take your eldest son, your firstborn son, and just cut him off!"

"Very well, Nick. That's fine."

Her hair was pinned now, and she rose and began to go away.

Nicholas sat still in his chair.

Rosetta spoke, almost to herself.

"Someone," she said, "has got to come in here to this house without emotion and do something about this. I think we need help."

Nicholas looked at her.

"No."

"All right, then," said Rosetta. "That's that."

She walked out of the room.

Hooker came in through the back of the house and passed his aunt in the hallway.

"Aren't you playing croquet?" she said. She looked surprised.

"No," said Hooker.

"Oh," she said. "Well, remember you're to be in bed by ten o'clock."

"Yes, Rosetta."

She turned in the doorway of her office.

"Hooker?"

"Yes?"

"When do you go to school again?"

"October."

"Well," she said distantly, "October. Well. Yes."

She sounded as though she was happy for him that he was going. Or was it that she was relieved? He could not tell.

The television set was turned on, but without the sound. On the few occasions he *did* watch, Hooker would watch like this, having to make up the story without hearing it. But this evening it was dull. It was always dull now. Nothing real ever happened. That one weekend it had been exciting.

"When was that?" he thought. "November."

Hooker pulled his knees up. A cowboy on the screen shot at and killed an old man. Hooker licked his kneecaps. They were dirty and tasted of rust

He closed his eyes. He tried to recall that Sunday morning. He saw the ambulance and the long hall and a lot of men lined up in a row. He could hear the low voice of the reporter, talking about Mr. Oswald and Mr. Kennedy and then Mr. Oswald was there, and then—

Mr. Oswald had funny eyes. He always looked angry, and once, on the Friday or the Saturday, he had said something very loud at the camera. Hooker had enjoyed it, because it was about taking a shower bath, and someone on the television set had laughed as well.

And then there was that other—that peculiar, brilliant second of time when the other man had run up out of the camera and poked his hand at Mr. Oswald, and Mr. Oswald had closed his eyes and made a shout, and people ran off in all directions, and somebody yelled, 'He's been shot! he's been shot! Oswald has been shot!' and in the library, Nicholas and Gilbert began to have an argument, and Rosetta turned the set off and told Hooker to get Iris to make some fresh coffee.

Now Hooker opened his eyes.

He looked at the screen. Some woman was smiling and holding a roll of toilet paper at him. He blinked his eyes and coughed and looked at her.

He thought, "Mr. Oswald has been shot. Go and get the coffee."

Then he thought, "I think I'll make some lemonade." He crossed to the television set and shut it off. "In November they shot Mr. Oswald. It was cold. We drank coffee. Mother came down. Now it's summer and the same old TV and hot, and mother—No," he thought, "I won't have lemonade. I'll just have ice water, instead."

In the kitchen, he ran up out of the crowd and poked his hand at Mr. Oswald, the ironing board. He made his own shout and fell on the floor.

"Mr. Oswald's been shot!" he yelled.

Iris came in.

"What the hell are you doing down there?" she asked, opening the refrigerator door.

"Dying," said Hooker.

"Dying! Ho! That's a laugh."

"I'm Lee Harvey Oswald," said Hooker. He groaned.

"Unh-hunh," said Iris. "Well, Mr. Oswald, unless you get up you can't have no ice cream."

"What kind?"

"Strawberry. I'm gonna take some out to Gilbert." She fished around inside the refrigerator.

"All right," said Hooker. "If I can carry all three plates."

He got up.

He brushed off the seat of his shorts.

Back by the porch they sat in a row and ate strawberry ice cream. It was cold, and they all made faces while they ate.

"Gilbert?"

"Yes?"

"What's assassinate really mean?"

"Usually it's killing for a bigger reason than plain ordinary murder. Like Kennedy and Abe Lincoln and the Archduke Ferdinand."

"Who was he?"

"A king. Not a king, but the next best thing. And they shot him at the start of the First War."

"Who shot him? Why?"

"A man. I think he was a student. Several people planned it, but the one man really did it."

"But why?"

"Well, they had to begin, you see, to get action, but they couldn't get it going. It was all political, anyway, and complicated. It had to do with sovereignty. So they decided what if they killed the Archduke, that would make something happen. Cause attention and division. So, it was for a political reason. Like Mr. Kennedy and Abe Lincoln."

Iris made a face.

"But they didn't have division after them," she said.

"No, but I think division was what they wanted. At least, that's what John Wilkes Booth wanted."

"Who was he?"

"An actor. He killed Abe Lincoln. Because he wanted to divide the nation over Mr. Lincoln's war."

"And what did Mr. Oswald want, then?"

Gilbert looked at his plate.

"Happiness," he said. "Same as Booth."

Iris and Hooker both watched.

"Happiness?"

"I think so," said Gilbert. "He thought that if he killed the President, then he could be happy, one way or another. Free, if you like that better. Some people say he did it for the Negroes, for instance."

Iris grunted.

"Others say he did it against the Negroes. You see? No one knows. Some say he was even a Communist. But whatever, I think it was really for his own happiness. He couldn't make the happiness—whatever it was—he couldn't make it happen unless he killed Mr. Kennedy."

Hooker was silent.

On the side lawn, the birds had gathered in the dusk.

"Aren't we ever going to know?" he asked Gilbert.

"No," was the reply, "never. 'Cause Oswald is dead himself, now."

After a minute, Hooker said, "I wonder if that made him happy."

Iris almost smiled, until she took a quick look at

Hooker and saw the expression on his face.

"Hon," she said very quickly, "you're spilling all your strawberry ice cream."

Hooker straightened the plate on his knee.

Gilbert said, "I don't know. I guess, if you're some people, it would make you happy, being dead. Especially if someone else killed you, so you wouldn't know it was happening. I don't know. I'd have to think about that."

"Did anyone ever make an assassination here?" Hooker asked, hoping that he could make a closer contact with the feeling, which was a feeling of people doing important things to each other—and making history.

"Not to the Prime Minister or to the Governor-General. But a man called D'Arcy McGee was assassinated. He was a politician."

"Where? Where?"

"In Ottawa. Someone shot him in front of the Parliament Buildings."

"Dead?"

There had to be death.

"Next best thing. He died from it later."

"And who did it?"

"I don't know."

"You don't know?"

"No one knows. Oh, they know—but they don't talk about it."

"Then it wasn't important"

"No, I guess it wasn't really important."

"Or we'd know about it."

"Yes."

"So there hasn't really been an assassination here?"

"Well, there was one, yes. Just not an important one, that's all."

The idea—the thought...the dream of closeness to it—faded.

They sat.

"I'll put these plates down for the cats when we're through," said Iris. "Right now it's best not to invite them onto the lawn 'cause of the birds."

"Look at them," said Hooker.

"There must be fifty of 'em there, or even sixty."

"You'd think there wouldn't be that many worms," said Hooker.

"Don't worry," said Gilbert. "There are."

He set aside his plate and drank from his glass of beer. "Uhg!" He belched.

"It's rude to burp," said Iris. "Excuse yourself."

"Excuse me," said Gilbert, and belched again. "I'm most frightfully sorry that I am forced to be so terribly rude all the time. At the Parkers' tonight I shall try to refrain from it."

"Oh, Jesus..." said Iris. "Christ!"

"I beg your pardon?"

"Be quiet and listen to the birds."

"I thought you said it was rude to listen in on other people's conversations," said Gilbert.

"It ain't rude to listen," said Iris, "when you don't know what they're saying."

They sat in the new dark, quiet.

"Like the birds..." she said.

"Hush."

Chapter 6

If you went into the lane, through the board gate in the fence, you saw a dirt and cinder-rutted road. Garbage cans and cinder pails marked off where the houses were. The Winslows were in the last house, and beyond their place the lane went on until it came to open country, and there it became a country road, hardly ever used except by children on bicycles, and, once a week, on Wednesdays, by the dump truck heading for the town dump with the garbage.

In the open, once it became a road and not a lane, there was a break in the fence, and if you crossed over to this break, going down into a ditch and up again, you would pass through into Winslow's Field. This was a long and narrow piece of land, used in the old days to pasture the horses. Now it was just a bumpy field, with a stream, a woods, and then more field, beyond all of which there was a high rise of hill which obscured every view of the distant city.

In the past, Hooker had gone on an average of three times a week. Now, favoring a lack of companionship—unless somehow, miraculously, it could be that Gilbert would take him somewhere or play with him—

he went there, alone, every day.

Some time ago, in the field beyond the woods, he had created a cemetery, in which he buried all the small animals—birds, mostly, and mice—that his cats had captured and killed. He buried each in an individual grave, and there were now about twenty of these. He also played back there in the field and in the woods.

When he made the graves, he made them quite shallow and never longer than a foot. His main intention was to get whatever had been killed safely out of sight and away into the earth where the cats could not get at it again. He thought of this as something he owed the animals, as a debt. But he was not sure of the reason.

On one particular day, Hooker came to the field with a small, dying squirrel in his hand. Phoebe, the wide-and-walleyed smallest of the cats, had brought it limply toward him as he was in the garden behind the house. She sat down with one paw on the squirrel's hind legs, while she held it, more lethally, by its neck in her mouth. She made a noise behind her clenched teeth. Hooker did not move. He was used to the mice and to the birds, probably because they were always dead. But here was something else—something still alive, something that looked at him.

He tried to get Phoebe to put the squirrel down. Gilbert looked on from behind the screen door on the back porch.

"Good Phoebe. Thank you, Phoebe. Go 'way, Phoebe."

Phoebe looked at him.

Gil belched. He was eating a peanut butter sand-wich, and he ate it with his mouth open, smacking his lips.

"Put it down," said Hooker. "Good girl."

Phoebe crouched and made little growls.

"Come on."

"Isn't she going to kill it?" said Gilbert.

"I don't know," said Hooker. "She's never brought me anything alive before."

"I'm sure she thinks she's very clever. Look at her damned eyes. Jesus!"

He went on eating.

"Put it down, Phoeb. Come on. Put it down."

Phoebe let go with her mouth and lay out flat, her ears forward, her paws resting on the squirrel, and her tongue stuck out between her teeth. Her eyes held on to Hooker's eyes. They looked excited—bright and different.

He advanced.

"Good Phoeb. Good Phoeb..."

Very quickly he bent down and took the squirrel away from her.

He looked at it.

Phoebe yowled.

"Bugger off," said Gilbert.

Phoebe paid no attention but focused still on Hooker, with that odd and different look of excitement.

"She's broken it," said Hook.

One of the squirrel's eyes was out and there was a long and deep gash, as though Phoebe had drawn her teeth through and down the length of the squirrel's neck.

"You'd better kill it," said Gilbert.

Hooker looked away.

"It doesn't need to die," he said.

"Sure it does," said Gilbert. "Look at its damn neck. It'll bleed to death if you don't kill it."

Hooker shuffled from one foot to the other. He had to go to the bathroom all of a sudden. His mouth dried up.

"I don't know how..." he said, looking at Gilbert. Gilbert looked faded behind the screen. He wiped his hands across his shirt.

"Kill it with the hatchet," he said. "That's quick."

"You," said Hooker.

"It's your damn cat," said Gilbert, apparently with a great deal of sense.

"But I don't know how!" Hooker wailed.

"Then it's time," said Gilbert, "that you learned how."

He disappeared, but his voice lingered a little, behind him:

"Time to get rid of those bastard cats. It's like patronizing Murder Incorporated or keeping a bunch of killers around here for damned amusement's sake. Why don't they ever kill each other? That's what I'd like to know."

Now Hooker could hear Gilbert and Iris in the kitchen, but it was not possible to tell what they said. He stood with the squirrel and tried to remember where the hatchet was. It was in the stable.

He went there and got it, putting it carefully into his wagon, where he also put an old piece of torn canvas from a decayed awning, and his burying spoon. This was a spoon relegated long before by Iris, for the express purpose of "cleaning up after those cats." Then he put the dying squirrel in a box, put the box on the wagon, and started off.

In the kitchen, Gilbert said, "There goes the wagon."

"Anh-hanh."

Gilbert looked out the window.

"This is like living in Belsen," he said.

"Where's that?" said Iris.

Gilbert stepped back and went to the refrigerator for a bottle of beer.

"Oh, well..." he said, giving a long and hopeless sigh. "Just a place, Iris. Nowhere but a place. That's all."

"Anh-hanh. Where's he got to now?"

"He's gone," said Gilbert. "He'll probably wait to kill it till he gets there."

"Poor lamb."

"Sure," said Gilbert. "Poor little Hooker."

He went off to the library, closed the door, and wrote "poor little Hooker" on a piece of paper. Then he looked at it and lay on the sofa thinking about it.

Hooker reached the trees.

Now he would have to kill the squirrel, and he looked at it. Its one eye, glassed over with terror, stared up at him watchfully. Hooker wondered how much pain it felt. It seemed beyond pain.

It looked at him. It stared at him, and it made a small noise, far up near its nose.

Hooker considered what must be done.

Around him, in the trees, some birds were quietly watching. And other squirrels were watching. Even the insects seemed to be quiet, and watching or listening.

With the spoon, he made way in the ground for the squirrel and put it down, alive, into the hole.

When he went to get the hatchet from the wagon, two crows flew off from a fir tree at the edge of the woods and swooped down, low, over the grave. Hooker ran at them with a noise.

"Go! Go! *GO!*" he screamed.

The crows flew up.

"Go—go! Go! Go! Go——go! *GO!*"

But they only clattered in the air around him, almost unafraid, shaking out the rags of their wings in his face, while he hunkered down over the hole in the ground, where the squirrel's eye looked up at him with a terrible calm, and he thought, "It's dead," before he saw that it moved, and then, because it startled him, he struck at it, all at once. Right down. With the hatchet. And the crows came over—whoosh!—and again—whoosh!— they came again, and went up, then, up and off and noisily into the spaces of the sky that were blue and unclouded, as though they must tell the woods there what they'd seen on the ground, while Hooker hit very hard and stopped and looked down into the hole and saw what he had done.

There was nothing there but a mess, which he covered with a piece of awning and threw in the dirt and petted it down with the spoon, very gently, not wanting to make an indentation.

And then he settled back, sitting very still.

He blinked in the direction of the trees where the crows sat. There seemed, now, to be a lot of excited talking.

He stared at them.

They flooshed out their wings and grawked at each other harshly, each probably blaming the other for having missed the free meal so neatly left there, lying on the ground. Their wings fluttered with a sort of petulant rustle and became quiet. They looked sharply from side to side.

Hooker sighed.

He wanted to lie down. He wanted to go to sleep, but the stare of the crows prevented him.

On the ground, over the newly turned earth, a procession of insect life, vast and varied, crisscrossed before him.

On the very edge of the grave he saw two dragonflies, one sitting on the other's tail.

Their wings were blue, like netting made of silver and steel, and their bodies were thin and black.

"He must be very weak," Hooker thought, "to have to lie there like that and let the other one carry him."

The eight wings began to beat and a low, resilient humming was produced, just before the two, glued into one, lifted themselves into the air.

Hooker knelt against the dampness of the earth and watched them fly away.

He wished that he had waved at them, their journey seemed so vast.

And then he rose and prepared to go home.

Around him, the field and the forest had begun to give off steam. He was aware of the heat of the sun. It burned his shoulder blades and made him thirsty.

The night before it had rained.

In the woods, the hatchet, jarred from side to side

by motion, made sparks against the metal fastenings of the wagon.

And this was the first of those rainless days that set that summer apart in everyone's mind as the worst and the hottest in memory.

Chapter 7

After supper, one evening quite early on in summer, Nicholas retired to the living room to read. Rosetta went into her office, and leaving the door open, which was unusual, she sat down at her desk and dealt with the accounts for the month of June. When she did this, she wore steel-rimmed glasses.

Looking in through the door, Hooker could see that the back of her dress was wet, although she sat very still.

He continued along the hallway until he came to the library. He could hear the forbidden television set. Gilbert. He opened the door.

"Have I got a cat in here?" he asked.

Gilbert, half sitting, half lying on the sofa, with a glass in one hand and a pencil in the other, gazed at him for a moment and then said, "No. Bugger off."

"What are you doing?" Hooker asked.

"I am watching TV." Gilbert pronounced each word exactly.

"With a pencil?"

"Will you get the hell out of here, Hooker? I'm going out later, and I only have a few minutes to be alone."

"What are you watching?"

The reply to this was a thrown shoe.

Hooker closed the door.

He continued his walk until he came to the foot of the stairs. He looked up at his mother's door. When would it open again? He sat down.

Iris appeared. She stepped out of the room with his mother's supper tray in one hand.

"You wanna come with me tonight?" she asked him. She carefully got onto the top step and then, sideways, came down the stairs one at a time.

"Where to?"

"It's Thursday, ain't it? I'm goin' to Alberta's."

"When?"

"Soon's I get those dishes done and change."

"All right," said Hooker. "I'll wait on you here."

"See that you do that, then. 'Cause it takes no time at all for me to get ready."

She passed on into the darkness toward the kitchen. The dishes, with half of Jessie's meal still on them, rattled to and fro as she went.

Hooker looked at his father in the living room. Beyond the green drapes, the room seemed cool and inviting. His father was apparently engrossed in his book. Hooker rose. All around him there was quiet.

He climbed the stairs and stood beside the door. He knew that it must be open, because the key had not been turned after Iris came out.

He tried the handle.

"Mother?"

The room was colored with evening light. It seemed shady and green.

His mother sat by the window in a chair.

"Who is it? Hooker?"

"Yes'm."

Jessica did not turn around. He could see that her crucifix, which was very old, lay on her lap, and her hands hovered over it. She was not a Catholic but had always owned a crucifix just the same. Now her hands quieted and fell, covering the cross and the figure it was hung with. A stillness came.

"What are you doing out of bed?" his mother asked him.

"I haven't gone to bed," said Hooker, "yet."

"Go to bed now, then. You mustn't get ill."

Hooker watched. Had she forgotten? Could she have really forgotten who he was—how old he was—what time it was?

"I said go, Hooker."

"Yes, ma'am."

He turned, and letting the door stand fully open, he said, "Couldn't I get you a glass of water or something, Mama?"

She shifted very slightly. Her neck revolved.

"No. Close the door," she said.

He watched her for one last second.

Her eyes closed. She paled.

"Go a—way!" she said. Her voice rose, and then she rose herself. "God—damn—you—Hooker! Get out of here!"

Clutching at the crucifix, she made her way toward him, as though she must be angry.

Why was she angry? What had he done to her?

Footsteps came into the hall below. Jessica's face was

a mirror of confusion. Hooker closed the door, suddenly finding that he stood beyond it, on the landing.

Quickly, the knob was wrenched from the other side, and he heard the key turn.

Rosetta came up to him, catching at her bosom as if she could force fresh air inside with her hands. Her eyes were exhausted with staring. She held him with one hand.

"Did you go in?" she whispered hoarsely.

"Yes."

"Oh, damn you, Hooker. Damn you."

She looked at the door. She looked at Hooker.

"Go downstairs at once. Go with Iris. Do whatever—but don't come back up here."

"Yes, Rosetta."

He went down a few steps.

"I mean it."

"Yes, Rosetta."

From the bottom he looked up and saw his aunt lean in impotently against the door, speaking softly:

"Jessie…Jessie…Are you all right, Jessie?"

Behind him, his father, who had come as far as the green drapes, made a clucking noise of disapproval but did not speak to him. He walked back silently, instead, to his chair and to his book.

Iris appeared.

"Alberta will be waiting. Come along."

Hooker allowed his hand to be taken. He looked at nothing. Without a word of departure they left the house and walked into the evening. They did not have far to go, but it seemed like a million miles.

"Won't I see her again, then, Iris?"

"Sometime."

"But when?"

"When it's right."

When it's right. When it's right. What on earth did that mean? It didn't mean anything. It meant nothing. Never. Never again?

They passed, like strangers, under the trees. The stars had begun to shine, but they were not pretty. They were too faraway. They seemed dangerous—like winter icicles.

Alberta Perkins was a large, very dark, colored woman; there was no mixture of blood in her veins. Once, she had been a deaconess in the Church. Like most other Negro servants locally she had been hired in the States by a visiting Canadian family.

Alberta had no sophistication. She needed none. She had always seemed a hulk to Iris—someone who sat in gigantic splendor, bearing the weight of an exiled sorrow across a huge and almost monstrous breadth of shoulder. Being a deaconess had given Alberta biblical grandeur. But now she had changed. She was no longer in the States. She was no longer in the Church. She was not the same. She drank now.

But Iris loved Alberta, no matter what she did.

Alberta had a quiet strength, which came from having once believed in God.

Alberta worked for the Harris family, in their large Victorian house, set back from Gate Street and completely hidden by a cedar hedge. It was popular among the children of the neighborhood to believe that Mr.

and Mrs. Harris had eaten their offspring—along with a large number of other children who had wandered onto the property, never to return. They had no other family save dead relatives in the graveyard and a son who had "fallen" in the First World War. Mr. Harris, now retired, had been a powerful man in Toronto, and he still sat on the board of a large firm downtown. Mrs. Harris wore clothes in the style of 1912 and could be seen on summer days walking her dog Teddy down the driveway, in the double shade of an orange parasol and a large flowered hat.

She was eighty-five years old—perhaps more.

At the moment, the Harrises were on vacation, and so, when Iris and Hooker approached the great darkened house, they went on over the lawn and up the steps to the front door, instead of around to the side.

Alberta met them and ushered them in.

"I got some pop for Hooker," she said. "It's in the kitchen."

They followed her through the hall to the back of the house, turning on lights as they passed.

"Darkness makes it cool," said Alberta.

In the kitchen, she gave Hooker a bottle of Pepsi-Cola, and they went on into the dining room.

They sat around the table, on which there had been placed a bottle of gin and two glasses.

"Oh, Lord! My people," said Alberta, easing herself from buttock to buttock, "is gone, like you know, to the lake. That lake there—Muskoka or what have you."

"Yes?"

"Yes."

Hooker squinted and listened.

"And they left me here in the town, 'cause I gotta take care of the dog. Can you imagine it?"

"Ho!" said Iris. "Too bad."

"Bad!" said Alberta. "Bad? I call it a human sacrifice. That's what I call it."

"It's so hot down here; it must be lovely at Muskoka, with the lake and all and the boats to row in," said Iris.

Alberta laughed. "Just give me the lake," she said. "In a boat, I'd drown."

Then they all laughed.

"Let me tell you 'bout the dog," said Alberta.

Hooker drank his Pepsi slowly and listened.

Iris lighted a cigarette.

"You see," said Alberta, "Mr. Harris figured it out that Teddy is old and will get sick up there or lost—or bit by snakes or go down and get attacked by some rabbit in a hole! So here—down here in the town—sits old Alberta Perkins, in the jungle steam of the summer, and where the hell do you think that ratty dog is at? Now where is he *at*? Guess. Go on. Just guess! Hooker?"

"I dunno," said Iris.

"I don't know," said Hooker.

Alberta looked at heaven and pounded the table.

"Where?" she cried. "Where?"

They did not answer.

"In the damn dogcatchers', that's where. In a cage!"

She made a hopeless gesture of age-old despair.

Teddy—like Alberta who served him and waited for him at the dog pound, who complained about him and hissed at him but who loved him nevertheless—was

old and fat and ugly. He was a dark-gray grizzled bulldog, probably twelve years old, whose favorite place to
lie was on top of people's feet. When the honored person chose to rise and move away, Teddy's eyes would
roll at heaven, and a long sigh would go up, just as
though his heart had been broken. Alberta always kept
tissues ready in her pocket, so that the moisture of
Teddy's kisses could be quickly wiped off and
deposited in the wastebasket. He was a sad dog, who
never really wanted to run away from Alberta, but who
found that his curiosity always led him into the hands
of the dogcatcher and eventually, through the apparently magical appearances of Alberta Perkins, back
onto the porch whence all his journeys from her presence began. Like wedded spirits, they seemed destined
to love one another, in spite of the fact that nature had
not intended them to marry.

Alberta drew the bottle of gin toward her across the
table.

"Time was," she said, "the dogs chased *us*!"

The lights about them were hooded with Tiffany
shades, and old mahogany gleamed at them on all
sides, from the massive backs of carved chairs and from
the polished surfaces of the table, a sideboard, and a
whatnot.

"Every damn day," said Alberta, pouring herself a
glass of gin, "every damn day, down I go to the lost-dog
place down there, and I say, 'Well, here I am again, Mr.
Dog Man—where's that little Teddy? An' here's your
two bucks.' So out comes Teddy, tail going fifty, with his
eyes all agoggle like that and *wah-wah-wah!*" Here she
barked. "To which I say, 'Hello, Teddy, you're a damn

nuisance, you little bugger,' an', 'See you tomorrow,' I says over my shoulder at the dog man. 'Sure', he says, 'see you tomorrow, Alberta,' an' I gets him home—Teddy, I mean—an' I puts down the biscuit. I puts down the milk. I pets him on the top of the head, an' he drinks. He eats. He yaps. He pees on the rug. So I says, 'Not in my house, Teddy—not in here. Out that door.' Hah! Yard? Now this yard here has got a fence that's five feet tall. Three sides, with the other side the house, y'see. And that damn dog is outa there in three minutes. Flat. Three minutes flat. I tell you." She paused. She reflected. Perhaps she remembered something. Then she said: "A kid's just the same, you know. Always runnin' away. Kids an' dogs alike. No fence, no love, no *nothin'll* hold 'em down. It's part of their gettin' on. You runned away once, didn't you, Hooker?"

Hooker shook his head.

"No? Well...someday." She winked at Iris. "Someday you will, boy. Mark my words."

She sighed and was quiet at last.

Iris looked at her.

"Not Hooker," she said. "Not Hooker."

"He's a boy; ain't he?"

"Certainly he's a boy."

"Well, then. It's natural's goin' to the john. With a *whoosh*!" She "flushed." "We has all run away, time to time."

"I guess so," Iris concurred. She looked at Hooker.

"They're funny people, them Winslows. That one I call the Deep Freeze, that Rosetta, she comes over here all the time, you know. Playin' bridge with the Harrises."

THE LAST OF THE CRAZY PEOPLE —

Hooker coughed.

"Go an' play," said Iris, and when Hooker had gone, she added, "Alberta! Honestly! In front of him."

"He don't mind," said Alberta. "Good God! He knows it, don't he?"

"Still," said Iris.

Alberta lighted a cigarette.

"This little boy's mother—there's somethin' about her, too, ain't there?"

"Yes."

Iris did not elucidate.

"Sounds like a swell place to live, all right."

"It's home," said Iris, trying to match Alberta's wit.

"Yeah. Home. Hunh."

Alberta reached for Iris' glass and poured some gin into it.

"Drink it up," she said. "Tell Alberta your troubles."

Iris fidgeted with the glass and swallowed a little gin.

"This little boy, Hooker, is different, all right," she said.

"You've said that about him before. What is he? Some kinda saint?"

"Of course not. But it's real strange, now I think of it, that he hasn't gone runnin' off."

"'Cause of the trouble?"

"Yes."

Iris drank.

"Of course," she said, "he's fond of his cats an' his field an'…me, I guess."

She smiled.

Alberta gave a horse laugh. She sat away back and shook.

"He likes yuh, eh? He really likes yuh?" she said.

"Yes," said Iris. To herself she said, "Not *me*—it's not me he likes but my *being* there."

"Hanh!" said Alberta. "It sounds like me an' Teddy." And again she laughed.

Iris paid no attention. She went on talking:

"I wish to hell you knew what it was like. I wish to God you did."

"Now, now, honey. Now, now."

"Well, I wish you did. What do you think it is like, bein' the maid to a bunch of people everybody thinks is nits? Havin' to go to bed in a house like that. Havin' to wash underwear for man who are downright peculiar. Havin' to take orders from somebody 't never smiles but always looks at you like you done—something."

"It's the condition," said Alberta. "That's the condition, honey, of bein' colored. What I always say—"

"Oh, God!" Iris said in desperation and anger, "I'm not talking about that!"

Alberta's eyes shifted away.

"There ain't ever been trouble, has there?" she said.

Now it was Iris' turn to snort.

"Ho!"

"Now, I mean real trouble, honey. Like that young man or somethin'."

"Gilbert? Gilbert!"

"Whatever his name is. Yes."

Iris thought, "She doesn't know what I'm talking about. She's living back in the States someplace. She doesn't even understand. Gilbert is always drunk... Gilbert is always out at parties, or asleep in the old library...Gilbert is always..."

"Alberta, you are old, and I think maybe you're wise. I have come to see you all these years, in this house. Can't you tell me how to bear it where I've got to stay? I been there maybe thirty years, now. And I can't go—I owe myself to them. To Miss Rose. I have to—live. With—them. Every day. People who—" She put her hands over her face, and her fingers moved. One hand finally dropped, and she tapped her words, one by one, onto the table. "These people are all asleep," she said. "Day and night. They lock themselves up in a bunch of old rooms. They make their whole life round things that are dead." She breathed. "In that Rosetta's office there's nothin' but pictures of old dead people—an' all Gilbert talks about is things that was the way they used to be. Always what's old. Always tryin' to make over the past. An' the old man! We hardly even speak. Alberta, don't you speak to Mr. Harris? Sure you do. But not me an' Mr. Winslow. I get called round the table—do this, do that—but I never gets to speak to him. An' he pays me my wages! At least, it's his money. It's Rosetta pays me."

She paused, closing her eyes, tight.

"And I'm always there, with the preparation in my mind that someone will die all of a sudden, or that someone else will get sick, or that Gilbert will end up in jail, or that Miss Jess will bolt her door somehow, and we can't get in, and she'll harm—herself. Death and sickness! And Miss Rose and I behave as hired nurses to them all, and I'm the only one for Hooker. The only time I ever—ever saw him happy, was so long ago I don't remember when it really was...."

She presented her face, with tears upon it, and

Alberta looked at her carefully. She picked up a deck of cards and proceeded to lay out hands for a game of rummy.

"You can always come here," she said. "The Harrises ain' here. An' this is an excellent brand of gin they serve."

"I don't want to get drunk. I don't want to be like you, old and ginny, drinkin' someone else's liquor without God. I don't wanta sit around the lousy dinin'-room table, playin' cards—forgotten!"

Iris stood up.

"I want Hooker, and I want peace, and I want to *know*. I want to know things."

The gin she had drunk went around and around inside her. She realized that she was saying something dangerous.

"I don't want to live with crazy people anymore."

She began to cry again.

"But I have to 'cause I have to. And there isn't anything I can do. I come here to this damn place, and nothin' happens. Here I am, is all."

"Sit down an' look at your hand," said Alberta. She herself played through and discarded. She was so calm, so big, and so immobile that the look of her figure, as she sat there, infuriated Iris.

"Damn you," said Iris. "Aren't you supposed to know anything? Why you sit there?"

Alberta tapped the table.

"I sit here because I'm old," she said.

"Old?" said Iris. "Old! What does that mean?"

"Sit down," said Alberta.

Iris sat.

"Pick up your cards."

"No."

"Pick up them cards."

Iris picked them up.

"Play."

"Then there isn't any answer," said Iris. "There isn't any answer."

"Drink the gin."

Automatically, Iris did as she was told. She perused her hand and played, discarding an ace. She lighted a cigarette. Her hands shook.

Alberta looked at the ace.

"Are you thinkin' right, girl?"

"I know what I'm doin'," said Iris. "I know what I'm doin'. I know what I'm doin'."

"Playin' off an ace at the top of the hand ain't good."

"I don't need it," said Iris. "Leave me alone. Let's play cards."

They were silent.

Far-off a clock was striking. It was nine o'clock.

Alberta made a grunting noise. She sighed.

"What is craziness in people, anyhow?" Iris said.

Alberta did not look up but wheezed over her cigarette. She droned a few words, looking at her cards.

She said, "Take all the people whole, honey. Put the craziness behind them where you can't see it, and get on living."

"But..."

"It's not your business, Iris. Just let 'em all range free."

"I can't watch that without knowin' what to do. I'm

scared, Alberta."

"You're just the maid, hon. That's all you are. The maid. An' a nigger to boot. You can't fight either one, for factuality. So give it up."

The Tiffany lamps burned hot and bright, gleaming with hardened color—orange...blue...green...red... purple...

"Yeah," thought Iris. "I play the colored maid— 'who said she wasn't afraid.' Hah! Just the way them Winslows play whatever it is they're always playing at."

"You gonna pick up that two o' spades?"

There was still lots to drink.

They sat there.

The living room was square and dark. The windows looked out from two sides of the house. The Harris furniture, their curtains, the whole flavor of the room was completely different from any part of the atmosphere in Hooker's house. Except, perhaps, Rosetta's office.

The chairs, the chesterfield, and one table were all covered with wrinkled gray sheets. Hooker had never seen this before. On one table, which was not draped in this way, there stood a photograph and before it, resting on a Chinese embroidered doily, there lay an old wooden box. The cover of the box was scratched and dusty. The photograph was of a sweet-eyed young man in a uniform. He could not have been more than eighteen. His hair was curly and dark. His eyes, even in the half-light which filtered through the gloom from the hall and the dining room, were large and luminous.

His mouth was small and full-lipped, and the expression on his face was that of someone who could remember only something sad.

Hooker opened the box.

Inside there lay a gun, a revolver, half-wrapped in a piece of purple silk.

Hooker watched the photograph. It must be fallen John Harris, the First War soldier. At his waist, neatly hung in its holster with the small brass catch, was this very gun that now lay in the box, looking cool and neat and useful.

Of course, John Harris had once used the gun. But it had not saved his life. With the gun in his hand he had fallen on the very last day of the War. The Old War. The first one. Everyone knew that. They all knew about Mrs. Harris and the telegram. They remembered how she had struck the delivery boy and how the boy had fallen onto the porch. Arnold Bamsdorf. Now he was a senior in the telegraph company. It was one of the town's stories, and you were told about it when you saw Mrs. Harris for the first time, walking her dog Teddy on the driveway. People said, "There is Mrs. Harris who knocked out Arnold Barnsdorf, because he brought the telegram about her son, on the last day of the War." Hooker looked at the gun.

"It killed someone," he thought "That gun. A German."

He reached in and picked it up.

It was quite heavy. Beside it, on the silk, there was a small box of bullets.

"Mr. Harris must keep it for burglars," Hooker thought.

91

It was oiled and clean and ready for use.

Hooker held it out, at arm's length, in both hands.
He drew in the trigger. The gun wavered. He turned in
a slow arc, sighting various gloomy chairs, and then,
pulling until the hammer clicked, he took a shot at the
photograph of John Harris.

The chamber revolved.

Hooker put the gun back down.

For a startled second he remembered that he had
not looked first to see if it was loaded. His palms
sweated. What if it had gone off? Well...it hadn't.

He ran his finger along the muzzle.

"I wish I had a gun."

He thought of the squirrel that Phoebe had hurt
and of killing it with the hatchet. He thought of the
crows and the dragonflies and the field.

"If I had a gun, I could kill them without hurting
them."

"What're you doin' there, honey?"

It was Alberta.

"Seeing the living room."

"But there's barely any light, child," she said,
switching on a nearby standing lamp.

The revolver gleamed like an enemy. It seemed to
tell Alberta that Hooker had lifted it out of its box.

"Don't touch that, Hooker. It's dangerous. Mr.
Harris keeps that for Arm'geddon...." Alberta chuck-
led and swayed, all ginny and tipsy, in the doorway.

"What's that?" Hooker asked.

"When everybody's gonna die. Don't you know
'bout that?"

"No. When? When is it?"

From the past she reached for the imaginary robe of her deaconess dignity—imaginary white, imaginary silk (it had really been sateen)—and with imaginary folds gathered in her empty hands, she swayed, as though standing before the Church lectern, and pronounced the beginning of her lesson.

"God is angry," she boomed.

The room caught at the words and held them, dustbound. The chairs in their sheets turned, it seemed, in the shadows to listen.

"No one knows, 'cept they knows it's coming. Arm'geddon..." She seemingly swiveled the whites of her eyes.

"God is angry," said Alberta dramatically. "And the sun and the moon and the stars get dark. The clouds will come, but it won't rain, and we will all—Mr. Harris, your daddy, and even your brother Gilbert—we will all be afraid. So will you.. ." she said, bending in toward him. "An' me—I will be, too. I will be afraid."

The curtain rings rattled across the old, hollow brass rod. Alberta stuck her head up. Her hands clutched at themselves in a prayer of fear.

"Outside," she went on, "the windows will show dead black, and every door will be shut tight, but none of that is gonna do no good." Her voice hushed low inside her, and the circles of her eyes grew wide. Hooker became quite alarmed. He watched her carefully.

She pronounced, "We shall all sit together. You. Me. And everyone. We sit in the houses, waitin'. A tiny little bird goes up with a screech...." It went up, personified by hands. "We all fall down under them tables there, and we are scared to death, and we hide." Pause.

"Hush! The wind has come, and the dust. An' now it storms all over around, and the earth comes open, and out of it now will come the dead, already dead, an' we will all be forced to be together, like it or not. An' now we will die again together." She coughed. The spell sank away in her eyes. "One by one. But all."

She stopped. She straightened up and smoothed her dress.

"It's a well-known fact," she said. "Some of us will die in pain, some will die in glory, and the sick among us will go easy into their death, and there will be"—a sigh, a pause, closed eyes; and then—"no more of suffering. The Bible says—I forgets where, but it does—that we will all meet up with God. His very self, an' that most of us will go to heaven. Most. Like for a moment it's gonna be real, real terrible, hon," she sighed. "But for those of us in this perdition *now*, it will surely be bless'd relief, and a glorious day of release."

"Perdition?"

"Hell. Like this is hell right here on earth. I mean"—she stared—"like it is for us. Me and the Nigras, Hooker. Or like it is for your mom and women. Like it was for John Harris and the sojers." She waved at the photo. She came awake and sober.

Alberta blinked into the living room.

What did she mean by that?

Hooker wondered.

Alberta began to compile a list.

"Like it is for Mrs. Harris," she one-toned, "after John Harris died so young. Like Teddy, like me and all unhappy dogs and people who"—she belched—"walk aroun' town or anywhere in pain. Like it must be for all the crazy people caught in madness. That is perdition. An' the answer to per—di—tion…" She slowed down, like a clock unwound. "…is merciful death, Hooker—sudden and unknown…." She looked at him. "Like I sometimes pray, on the street downtown, a brick'll fall on my head. So's I don't have to think about it. Pow! Dead. Like that." She gazed off into the house. "Now, what'd I come in here for?"

She blinked back at Hooker. Her black face gleamed and looked purple in the odd light. She perspired. Hooker could smell the gin.

"You don't un'erstan'—do ya, honey?" she said. "You just don' un'erstan'."

Hooker looked back at her. She smiled.

"I do a little," he said.

But that was a lie. He understood it all. Even about the brick downtown, and Teddy.

Chapter 8

On Jessica's birthday, late that July, they decided to see if she would finally come downstairs in the evening. She had been inside her room, by then, for three months.

That afternoon, Iris ordered ice cream, which Harry Jarman delivered in a box of dry ice, and she made a large angel-food cake with icing.

They hurried through supper and gathered in the living room for dessert and coffee.

Nicholas had laid a fire, which was traditional.

He said, "Whatever you say, it's the only good way to get rid of the wrappings." But usually Rosetta would manage to save the wrappings and the cards, and she always saved the ribbon.

This evening, Jessie's presents were arrayed on the far end of the sofa. She would sit and undo the packages there.

There were two presents from Nicholas, two from Rosetta, one apiece from the boys, and another from Iris. Two or three of Jess's nearly forgotten friends had called, bringing presents, in the morning, but she would not talk to them or let them see her. She had dismissed her friends, and now they were beginning to dismiss her.

"That fire is ridiculous," said Rosetta. "We'll roast to death."

"But we always have a fire," said Hooker. "Every birthday."

"Jess will like it," said Nicholas. "She's used to it. We want to make her comfortable."

"Well, don't put on any more logs," said Rosetta. "Or you'll just make us *un*comfortable, Jess included."

They all sat down.

Rosetta rang for Iris to bring the coffee tray, and while they waited for this, she said, "Now, Gilbert. Knock at the door and say 'Happy Birthday.'"

Nicholas laughed.

"He knows what to say, Rose, don't worry."

Hooker sat forward in his chair.

"Can't I go, too?" he asked.

"No. We don't want a lot of noise and fuss. If she sees that we're all nice and quiet and relaxed, then she'll come down."

"But I haven't seen her, either," said Hooker.

"You'll see her just as soon as we will, dear. Now, go on, Gilly. And remember, nothing has changed or is different, at all."

Gilbert grimaced, rose, and went into the hall, where he paused at the foot of the stairs. He had not had a drink all afternoon. He had bathed and rested, and now he wore a clean white summer suit and a brand-new tie. He began to go up.

They listened.

Gilbert knocked at the door.

Words.

Nicholas fidgeted with his handkerchief and lighted a cigarette. He looked into the flames and absentmind-edly broke the match he had used into several small pieces.

Iris arrived, carrying a large silver tray, which she placed on a table in front of Rosetta's chair.

"You might as well stay, now," said Rosetta. "After she's opened her things, you can get the ice cream and cake."

"Okay," said Iris. "I'll just stand over here, then."

She took up a place at the end of the sofa nearest the door—the end at which Jess would sit.

They heard a noise in the hall, and they all turned to watch.

"She's coming," said Hooker. "She's coming. She's coming."

"Now, dear, you must be quiet," said Rosetta.

Nicholas gripped the arms of his chair.

Out on the stairs they could see Jessica.

She was dressed in a green robe and wore a ribbon, which tied back her hair.

"I won't fall," she said, "will I?"

"No, Mama. I'll help you."

"This is too exciting," she said. "Much too exciting."

"She's smiling," said Hooker.

"Iris, do make him be quiet."

"Come on, Hook. Shut up. We want your mom to be able to relax."

Hooker closed his mouth.

Gilbert and Jessica reached the bottom step and turned toward the living room.

Nicholas rose, and Hooker, goaded by Iris, followed

suit. Even Rosetta stood up.

Gilbert brought Jessie all the way to the doors, and then he stepped back so that she could come in alone.

"Nicky!" she said.

Her voice was surprisingly quiet, like a hermit's—someone whose voice must only reach his own ears.

Nicholas crossed the room and kissed his wife on the cheek. She withdrew from this gesture slightly, but it was barely noticeable.

"Rosetta," she said. "And a fire. Isn't that lovely?" She was still inaudible. "Isn't that lovely?"

They all waited.

"Hello, Iris."

"Hullo, Mrs. Winslow. Nice to have you come down."

Jessica put out her hands. Iris helped her to the sofa. She sat.

They waited again.

Suddenly Jessica looked up and said, absolutely out loud, "Gilbert. Gilbert came all the way upstairs and brought me down. Did you know that?"

Rosetta smiled and said, "That was nice, dear."

Jessica looked at the little pile of gifts beside her and said, "Isn't that pretty. Packages like that. I like that. I really like that."

Rosetta said, "Why don't you open them, dear?"

"I will," said Jessica. "I will."

But she did not open them. Yet.

Instead, she seemed to lapse for a moment into some sort of reverie.

Everyone watched her, and eventually Rosetta spoke:

"What are you thinking about, Jess?"

"What?"

"You were dreaming, dear. What were you thinking?"

"I wasn't dreaming, Rosetta. Don't accuse me like that, all the time. I wasn't dreaming at all. I was just sitting here. Simply sitting here. Can't I do that, if I want to?"

Hooker, who still had not been acknowledged, edged closer to Iris.

Jessica said, "Nicholas. I wasn't dreaming. Was I? I was just sitting here. That's all. Tell her—"

"Rosetta wasn't criticizing, dear. She was only interested—"

"She said I was dreaming."

"Well, she didn't mean any harm, Jessie. She didn't. Really."

Jessica took a deep breath. Her eyes narrowed.

"You always take her side. Don't you? She can't do anything wrong. Neither could your damned mother."

She looked at Rosetta.

"That's my coffee service," she said.

"Yes, dear. Of course it is."

"And this is my house."

"Yes."

"Well? Well? Why is my coffee service in front of you? I'm not incapable, you know."

"Now, Jess. If you want to pour, of course you may. We just thought you'd be happier opening presents and not having to fuss. That's all."

"I don't want to pour."

They waited, but nothing further was said about it. Instead, Jessica, momentarily retiring from the

situation, sat quite still again and looked at her slippered feet. Her face reflected an intimate and delicate
confusion.

Finally she said, "Well, what's in the boxes?"

Rosetta said, "Open them. See."

"Are you sure they're all for me?"

"Yes, of course. It's your birthday, isn't it?"

Jessica reached out. She chose Gilbert's package.
Very slowly, she undid the ribbon and then the box
itself.

"Oh, Gilly. It's stockings, but I never wear stockings
anymore."

Gilbert smiled.

"They're to wear downstairs," he said.

"Downstairs?"

"Yes."

"But—"

Rosetta spoke quickly:

"Open another one, Jess."

"Which? Which one?"

"That one. Why not open that one?"

"It's so tiny."

Jessica delicately pulled away the paper from a
small, celluloid-covered box.

"Balls," she said.

There was a moment of silent confusion. Nicholas
blushed.

"Bath balls," said Jessica. "Oil. How pretty. How did
they get here? Who brought them?"

"I did," said Rosetta. "They're wonderful. They're
scented. Just put one in your bath, and it dissolves
itself. They color the water, too. Lovely smells. Like—

lavender, rose…"

Jessica watched her, holding the package of bath balls with care.

"I use soap."

Rosetta laughed, very lightly—unsure.

"These are as well as soap, dear. Just scent, that's all."

"I use soap that's scented."

"I know, dear."

"Then why did you give me these?"

"Because they're pretty, dear."

Jessica laid them aside.

"Oh," she said. "Oh. And what's this?"

With a sigh of relief, Rosetta sat back.

"I think that's from Nicholas."

It was a large, store-wrapped box with a bright red ribbon. Jessie lifted it onto her lap.

"And this?"

Rosetta leaned forward to look.

"Oh, that's just another little thing from me, dear."

"Another? Two presents. Really, Rosetta!"

She tore away the paper.

"Lipstick."

Her face took on a look of childish misdemeanor.

She uncapped the ornate, carved, golden tube and looked at the little red rod of color. She twisted it open.

"It reminds me," she said, "of something." Working the dial at its base, raising and lowering the small red tongue of coloring. "Isn't it funny," she said, and smiled directly at Nicholas.

Then all at once the lipstick rose to her face, and she drew an incoherent mouth around the outlines of her lips.

Rosetta gasped.

"There," said Jess. "Oh! It smells so," she said.

"Don't—"

Gilbert lowered his head. They waited, but the word remained unattached.

She let the lipstick fall into her lap. Immediately she opened the package from Nicholas.

Gilbert did not watch at all, now. He sat with his head bowed, his hands dangling down between his legs.

Nicholas frowned. He wanted to look at Rosetta, but he could not make his head turn in her direction. His eyes were fixed on his wife, who sat now, clown-colored, opening his present. He knew that inside the package she would find his traditional offering of a plain blue nightgown with white needlework at the collar. His hands, involuntary wardens of the purity of his intentions, stretched out to guard his gift from what they must all now conclude.

"Nick. Oh! Nicky!"

She lifted it out of the box into the full view of the family.

Hooker thought it was pretty.

"It's—Why did you? Why did you? It's—"

The accused nightgown fluttered in her grasp.

"—a bride's nightie." The words tumbled about the room without coherence except in Nicholas' mind.

She let the nightgown fall, and her voice became a specter of itself as she spoke.

"What are you trying to do to me?" she said plaintively. "What are you all trying to do? Don't you understand why I am sick?" she said. "Isn't that clear?"

She looked from face to face. Even to Hooker, who stared back at her—alarmed, afraid, and ignorant.

Jessica's head turned violently away.

"I won't sleep with you, Nicky," she said. "Ever again. You know that. You know it. And I hate you for this."

Gilbert coughed inadvertently.

They all looked at him.

Jessica stood up.

Nicholas said, "Jessie—Jessie, please…" meaning to say "please sit down" but she turned on him with that other interpretation which was so ready, now, to fall on everything he said.

"No." Her voice rose. "No. No babies. No babies. No babies."

She reached out and was caught by Rosetta.

Rosetta said, "Iris. Get Hooker out of here. Call Dr. Deems."

Iris, gathering Hooker on her way, escaped around Jessica's clutching hands and made for the kitchen.

Nicholas said, "Gilbert, help your aunt."

Gilbert said, "No."

"What?"

"No."

Jessica, by now escorted to the stairs by Rosetta, was saying, as though in careful explanation of some previous act of violence, "Blankets…pillows…bathtubs…"

"Now, dear." Rosetta helped her gently.

"Stairways…"

"Now. Now. Now. Now."

"I'm afraid. I'm afraid. I will. I know I will."

"That's all right, dear. It's all right. You can't. Don't

you remember? The baby is already gone, Jess. Already dead. It died in April."

"Why does he have to be mean? Why are you all so mean? I tried to explain it. I did really try. But I can't. Doesn't he understand?"

Their voices drifted up toward her room, becoming quieter as they went and less afraid and more assured of safety. Finally, with a click, the door removed them altogether.

In the living room, Nicholas looked at Gilbert.

"Why wouldn't you help her?" he said.

Gilbert sat quite still and finally looked up at his father with a wavering stare; but his head did not rise to the occasion—only his eyes.

"I was just thinking," he said, "that it's pretty damn funny that you were the man who told me about sex."

"That's certainly a help," said Nicholas. "Thanks."

"I'm sorry," said Gilbert, standing up and preparing to go to the kitchen. "I'm sorry. It's just—I didn't really understand all this before, but now I do. Dad—I really thought she was an invalid when she came home, but now I don't think she is." He paused. "I think we are."

"Explain yourself."

Gilbert turned in the doorway, his white suit stained with perspiration.

"If I could, you wouldn't love *me* anymore. Or you wouldn't need me," he said. He smiled. "The way she doesn't need you." He gestured at his mother's door. "That," he said, "is what happens when you explain yourself."

He walked away down the hallway and into the kitchen.

Nicholas came to the drapes and stood looking up the stairs.

"But, it was only a *present*," he said to himself aloud. "Just a perfectly ordinary present. A gift. It didn't mean anything."

"Doctor's coming," said Iris.

"Of course he is," said Nicholas. "Naturally."

In the kitchen, Clementine, a large red cat who was currently expecting kittens, lay in the center of the floor.

Hooker said, "Get out! Get out! You can't have babies here!"

He threw a tea towel at her, and she ran away under the table.

Gilbert said, "She'd better not have her damn kittens near me, that's for sure!"

Clementine, reappearing courageously, lay down in front of Hooker on the floor and rolled over, purring. She was much slower now than she had been, and her pregnancy had begun to show. She was almost alarmingly fat. For a young cat—she was a year old now, and this was to be her first litter—she looked also surprisingly mature, and had developed an array of traits of wisdom and of caution that were almost comical when she was in the company of the other cats. She seemed at least five or six years older.

"It takes all mothers like that," said Iris. "It gives 'em that haughty look. You know? Kind of, 'Look at me, buster, I know a thing or two that you don't know.'" And then Iris laughed, but Hooker did not laugh with her. Gilbert did.

"That's a lie," Hooker said. "It doesn't take them all like that. It made my mother hide, but Clementine runs around in front of everybody."

"Well, that's the way it should be, hon. A pregnancy is nothing to be ashamed of."

Gilbert grunted.

Iris brushed some cat fur off her uniform.

"Who's for a beer?" said Gilbert.

"Me," said Iris. "Everyone be damned. We gotta sit here and wait for Dr. Deems, anyway."

Gilbert fussed at the refrigerator.

Iris and Hooker sat down.

Hooker looked at Iris and said, "If she doesn't open my present, it will spoil."

"No, it won't, hon," she said. "It'll keep."

"No," said Hooker, "it won't. It was a bird's egg, meant to hatch a robin."

He folded his hands on the table.

Gilbert was opening the beer.

"HON—EY!" said Iris. "Honey? A robin's egg. S'posed to hatch? You're kiddin' me. You know better'n that."

Hooker looked up, confused.

"Why?"

Iris accepted the beer from Gilbert.

"Well, no robin's egg is gonna hatch in any old box up in someone's bedroom. It's gotta have a—"

She stopped.

"What?" said Hooker.

Iris looked over her shoulder. Her tone softened. She faced him again.

"A nest," she said. "It's gotta have a nest. That's all."

Hooker nodded.

"Oh," he said.

And Gilbert just looked out the window.

Chapter Nine

On one of the hottest days, that long hot summer, a little gossip broke out somewhere in the city, but Hooker did not understand it when it happened. Later, of course, there were events that he could gauge it by, and he did understand, but not at first, not right when it happened.

The way Hook heard about it was this: Nicholas came back one day, earlier than usual, from the city. It was about three o'clock in the afternoon, the lonely time when Gil, Rosetta, Jessie, and even Iris dozed in their appointed places—library, office, bedroom, and kitchen. Hook was sitting on the stairs, holding Little Bones.

The front door opened.

Nicholas came in. Hooker watched him, unseen. Little Bones had been ill all morning with a vomiting disease, and she was cradled asleep in his lap, one paw draped over his arm, and he did not want to disturb her. So he remained silent.

"Rose!" said Nicholas.

Silence.

"Rose!"

Far away down the back hall, Rosetta's office door

opened, and she emerged, from what had obviously been a very deep sleep.

"Nicholas? Nick?"

"I'm in the hall."

She came through to him.

"Dear..." She almost ran. "What is it? What is it?"

Quickly she divested him of the overcoat, the hat, the cane, and the gloves. He stood there, looking naked in his suit.

"Nick. What's happened?" she said. "Come into the living room."

"Bring some sherry," said Nicholas. "Quickly."

He handed over the key unceremoniously. Rosetta already had her hand on her own keys, which rested in the pocket of her dress. She stood for a moment with keys in either hand. She would, of course, use his.

She went to her office.

Nicholas blew his nose and walked into the living room, fumbling his way through the green drapes like a man in a dense fog.

Hooker sat still.

Rosetta came back. She carried two glasses and the sherry bottle, pulled the drapes, disappeared, and pulled them back into a closed position. They swayed heavily.

Veiled voices drifted into the hall and up the stairway:

"Gilbert's in trouble."

"Oh, Nick..."

"He's in trouble with..."

"What?"

"Mrs. Varley told me."

"What's it to do with her?"

"You know her—she has all those artificial, artistic friends. She was married to Jack."

"Jack Varley."

"Of course."

Hooker heard the cork being pulled, and the sherry being poured...once...twice. Gilbert was in trouble. What had happened?

"She had a party—last night."

"Last night?"

"Last night."

Sounds of drinking. Sounds of pouring

"She didn't invite him, but he was there."

"Gilbert?"

"At Mrs. Varley's."

Sounds of muted coughing.

"But surely her friends must be older than he is."

"Well, she hadn't invited him—do you understand?"

"Yes. Yes. I understand. She hadn't invited him—"

"But he was there."

"Yes?"

"And all her friends are very wealthy. And all of her friends were there."

Significant pause.

"All of them there. Yes?"

"Some of her friends are men downtown. Do you see?"

"Oh, God! Your friends—"

"In my club...on the street..."

Sounds of drinking. In Hooker's arms, Little Bones began to stir.

"Well..."

"One of these men—thank God I don't know him—but he has—"

"Yes?"

"A daughter."

There was absolute silence.

"What's his name?"

"Parker. His girl's name is Janice."

"No!"

"Yes."

"No. Not Janice Parker!"

"Yes."

"And our Gilbert?"

"Right."

"Oh, my God!"

"And at this party, Mrs. Varley says she's never been so terribly shocked in her life. She says it was so indiscreet. She says there was talk—right out loud, mind you—about Janice Parker and—Gilbert."

Little Bones struggled out and onto the step by herself, sitting there, independent but woozy. She shivered.

"What have we done? What have we done?"

"She's going to Jamaica."

"Are you certain, Nick. Have you checked?"

"Yes. I telephoned this morning. I telephoned the Parkers."

"But what did you say?"

"I asked to speak with her."

"Nicholas!"

"It was all right. I didn't say who I was."

"Well?"

"She'd gone—last week."

"Thank God for that."

"Yes. She's gone. And nothing outright has been said, yet. At least, nothing but that damn man at the party."

There was more drinking, and Hook could hear them both settling further into their chairs. Little Bones began to shake all over and to heave. Hooker put his hand on her back, near her tail. She went on heaving, silently.

"What are we going to do?"

"Nothing."

"But Janice Parker is only eighteen."

"She's seventeen."

"Poor girl. Not having a mother, and now—"

"It's par for the course. Par for the course. And naturally, it all comes straight back at us."

"Yes, dear."

Little Bones gave a cough. Hooker said, "Shhh."

"Mrs. Varley said she felt it was her duty to let me know. She said it wasn't common gossip, but it was certain enough. She had heard Gilbert's name."

"Well, all I can say is, Mary Varley has lots of brass. Just to pick up the phone and tell you about it like this."

"The only trouble is, God knows who was at that party. Anybody could have been there."

"It's too good to miss. First Jess and now Gilbert."

After a moment, Hooker heard Rosetta's voice again:

"Poor Hooker."

Hooker leaned forward.

"Hooker?"

"Yes."

Pause.

"What are we going to do? What if she sues? What if she sues him?"

"She'd have sued him by now if she was going to."

"It isn't right. No. It's not right. He's going to get off scot-free. My God—it's almost a joke."

There was a sound of silence.

"He probably doesn't even know."

"Of course he knows."

"Now, now."

"This is what you get for giving him that damn car!"

"Well, he's not going to drive it anymore."

"I told you. I told you. We've got to do something."

There was a sound of shuffling. Rosetta had begun to straighten the furniture and to fuss with the room.

"I don't understand—I will never understand you, Nick."

Little Bones threw up.

Rosetta approached the other side of the curtains. Nick's voice followed her.

"Still, I don't think we should say anything."

"And I suppose we're expected to pray that Mary Varley will shut up?"

"Yes."

"Shotgun! They're going to hold a shotgun over your son, and you just sit there!"

Rosetta came through the curtain. She was adjusting her hair net and had a pin in her mouth. Her face was pale and hard and ugly.

Hooker trembled. Shotgun?

"I wonder what it will be," said Rosetta.

"I hope to God we never know the answer to that," said Nicholas.

Rosetta looked blankly at her brother and then walked down the hall toward her office.

Hooker lay along the step, holding onto Little Bones with both hands. She was beginning to heave again.

He got up, and leaving her there with her mess on the stairs, he went down to the hall and straight out, unheard, through the front door and around to the alley. Shotgun.

Gil lay in the bathtub.

Beside him, on the turned-down toilet lid, was a glass of cheap red wine and a bottle.

He was reading:

"Behold," he read from a green-covered book,

> "Two score and ten there be
> Rowers that row for thee,
> And a wild hill air, as if Pan were there,
> Shall sound on the Argive sea,
> Piping to set thee free."

He drank, settled a little, and read on:

> "Or is it the stricken string
> Of Apollo's lyre doth sing
> Joyously, as he guideth thee
> To Athens, the land of spring;
> While I wait, wearying?"

Outside the door, Gulliver, Hooker's dog-faced cat, began to scratch for admittance. The words went on:

"Oh, the wind and the oar…"

Gilbert paused and closed his eyes. "Oh, the wind and the oar…," he said aloud. Gulliver scratched. His paw appeared through the crack under the door.

"Bugger off!" said Gilbert.

> "Oh, the wind and the oar,
> When the great sail swells before,
> With sheets astrain, like a horse on the rein;
> And on, through the race and roar,
> She feels for the farther shore.
>
> Ah, me,
> To rise upon wings and hold
> Straight on up the steeps of gold
> Where the joyous Sun in fire doth run,
> Till the wings should faint and fold
> O'er the house that was mine of old:
> Or watch where the glade below
> With a marriage dance doth glow."

Gil smiled, drank, spilled wine on his chest, and read on, oblivious for a moment, not even hearing Hooker's emissary at the door.

> "And a child will glide from her mother's side
> Out, out, where the dancers flow:
> As I did, long ago."

And now he paused and held the book away, over the edge of the tub. He drank some more wine, and spilled some more, and thought of the final lines with his eyes closed tight and his toes treadling in time against the weight of the water.

> "Oh, battles of gold and rare
> Raiment and starred hair,
> And bright veils crossed amid tresses tossed
> In a dusk of dancing air!"

"Oh, Youth," he said inside himself, "and the days that were!"

He let the book fall. It made a spluttering noise of folding and wounded pages on the tile.

Slowly, note by note, he began to hum some tune or other, a bit of this, a bit of that, some old tunes he had heard a long time ago from Iris—for Iris was his childhood singer, too—and he finished what was in the glass he held, and as he rolled toward the bottle on the toilet, he saw that the water he lay in was red.

"Now that's too bad," he said. "I'm going to bleed to death."

He poured out more into the emptied glass and lay further up so that now he would not spill it. A few little twists of steam rallied from the bath water. Gulliver scratched, almost frantically. There was a long moment of suspended animation. Gil stared at the steam and at himself and at the mildly colored water.

"Shall sound on the Argive sea..." he said.

"Oh, Youth and the days that were."

Gulliver bunted impatiently at the door.

"Get away from there, damn you!" Gilbert shouted.
He threw the book at the door.

"Is it impossible to be allowed to think?" he thought.
Someone said, "Gil!"

Gilbert, thinking of Gulliver, was dumbfounded.

"Come out of there."

"Why? I'm taking a bath."

"Well, get out at once. We need you. Hooker has disappeared, and no one knows where."

"Oh, for Christ's sake," Gilbert muttered, "I'd rather stay here and bleed."

When he opened the door, Gulliver meowed at him plaintively.

"Some people," said Gilbert, "will do anything for attention. Get out of my way."

But Gulliver, watching the dripping, towel-draped figure retreating down the hall, only looked at him casually, without fear, and then went inside the bathroom, where he watched the tinted water disappearing down the drain.

They had not discovered that Hooker had gone until it was nearly suppertime. Everyone said, "Where is Hooker?" and, nobody knowing, they immediately thought, "He has gone to the field," or, "He has gone down the alley," or, "He has gone hiding in the stable." These things had all happened before.

When they had gathered in the hall, Rosetta, standing at the foot of the stairs, said, "Well, I must say, I thought Hooker was the one member of this family we didn't have to worry about. But I was obviously wrong."

Apparently without noticing that Gilbert had come down the stairs and was standing behind her, she said, "This house smells like a brewery!" and walked away down the hall to telephone the police.

Gilbert said, "Oh, all right, for Christ's sake, I'll get on his bike, if it's there, and go and look in the field."

Iris, acknowledging Rosetta's remark with a pointed glance at Gilbert, said, "I'll look down the alley."

Gilbert went out to the stable and got the new, blue bicycle. Hooker hardly ever used it. Aside from his wagon, he was not particularly vehicle-proud or speed-conscious. He had gone with his father to the sports store and looked. When he had seen one that was blue, he had said, "That one." It had been that simple. Nicholas had had a man put it in the rear of the car, and they had come home. When Gilbert had seen that it was blue, he had smiled. Now, again, he smiled as he took it up. A kid's bike and blue—like the one he'd never had.

He wheeled it out through the board gate and into the alley. He bent down to tuck his trousers into his socks, and as he did so, he could see that Iris was moving off on foot in the opposite direction. Every once in a while she yelled out, "Hook! Hooker! Hook— Hooker!" and peered up over a fence. He smiled at her thin, strange back, her bony arms and legs. And then he got on the bicycle.

He rode off down the lane. His knees stuck out as he rode. He tried, once, riding without using his hands, but the road was bumpy, and he almost fell. He got to the hole in the fence, took the bicycle through, and tramped off toward the woods.

He lighted a cigarette and watched around him as he went.

It was a pretty place. It smelled pretty, he thought— it had the smell of tall grass, grass that was dry now, and there was the smell of trees, too, and the smell of warm dust. He looked down and saw that there was dust on his shoes. "I should have put on my other clothes to come here, damn it all," he thought. Then he began to walk carefully, lifting his feet higher as he went on over the stream and into the trees.

Here it was almost dark, but the path was clear and quite apparent. He could see where Hooker had dragged the wagon on all his countless trips.

"Bury the dead," said Gilbert out loud, looking down at the wagon tracks. "What a funny kid. Imagine. All this way just to bury a bunch of mice and a few screwed birds."

He looked all around in the middle of the woods, quietly smoking, forgetting why he had come.

"It's certainly lonely here," he thought. "It's certainly lonely." And then an unaccountable thought came to him. Suddenly, and with the prompting of a physical shiver which crossed over his shoulders, he thought, "Like a place to die." For a literal second only he came to a full stop, in the dark, and then walked quickly and with just the vaguest memory of his direction and purpose, right out through the woods to the field.

Immediately, all the birds flew away, and he saw the sky filled up—as Hooker must so often have seen it— with wings and bodies, with furious figures darting off and away to the edges of the darkening trees. Gil felt a sense of consecration.

It was there in the field. But he could not explain it. Not holy—not like that. But in some way consecrated to a purpose.

"It's cold here," he thought.

Then he went back, for he had not found Hooker.

Rosetta dialed the police number on her desk telephone.

She said, "This is Rosetta Winslow speaking. I'm calling for Nicholas Winslow. We have lost a little boy. No. Miss Winslow. I am Nicholas Winslow's sister. That's right. Yes, Miss Winslow. We live on Perry Avenue, right at the end."

There was a pause.

"Well, he's ten. His name is Hooker."

There was another pause, and Rosetta made a face.

"Hooker Winslow. This is Rosetta Winslow speaking, and I'm phoning for Mr. Nicholas Winslow. Thank you. Eight forty-nine Perry Avenue. Perry three, two-eight-six-nine. Two-eight-six-nine, yes. Brown. Green. Around four feet. Tan-colored shorts. Blue shirt. Running shoes and no socks. That's right—*Hooker*."

After the next pause she said, "Mr. Winslow, my brother, will be down shortly. Yes. Thank you."

She hung up.

Nicholas was standing in the doorway

"Well," she said, "they're going to send a car out looking for him. I told them you'd be right down. You will go right down, won't you?"

She went to the closet to get his things.

"Ten?" she thought. "Ten? Or is he eleven?"

The late afternoon sun did not impart its light onto the walls of the Harrises' house. Shadows, instead, moved on the lawn and clambered up the trellises and over the shutters toward the roof.

Hooker wondered how he might get in.

He could ring the bell. Alberta would come. She would ask him what he wanted, and because she was Alberta, Hooker would have to tell her. Naturally, he could not do that.

And what about Teddy? Was he there? Would he bark? Hooker would have to be very careful.

He stood by the cedar hedge and looked across the lawn. How cool it was. And then he heard the hose.

He could not walk down the driveway because the gravel would make noises and give him away. And so he stepped onto the grass.

The watering noises became louder, and he figured that it must be someone at the back of the house. Perhaps Alberta was watering the yard, and if she was, then it was practically certain that Teddy would be sitting there with her, on the back steps.

Hooker got onto the front porch. The door stood open beyond its screen. For a moment he continued to listen to the sounds, and then, when he heard that Albert was singing back there, he was sure that it would be safe to go in.

He did.

The screen door clicked twice as he went through, closing it behind him.

To get into the living room, he had to turn a corner in the hall, and there the living room and dining room faced each other, divided by a Turkish rug and the figure of Teddy, sound asleep.

Hooker stared at him. He could smell the dog and also other things—wicker and dry curtains and orange peel. The whole house smelled old, and it was the composite odor that Hooker associated with the times before he was born—with the wars and with long dresses and with the dead people that you saw in photographs. It had to do, too, with the smell of waxed banisters and the smell of rugs when you lay on the floor to read the funnies. Not many houses had this smell. His own house had it in some rooms, and the Harrises' house seemed to have it all over.

He stepped past Teddy and went into the living room. The old bulldog lay so still that if he had not been breathing, he might have looked dead. But his mouth was open, and his tongue lolled out, and his eyes flickered in a dream. Hooker knew that Teddy's bark was very loud and that, if he woke up, he would have hysterics because of his great age, and Alberta would come, and she would call Iris, and Iris would tell Rosetta, and Rosetta would tell the Harrises, and the Harrises would have him put in jail for robbery.

Beyond the curtains in the filtered dark, Hooker stopped and thought of Armageddon and of shotguns.

What light there was came through the shutters in strips and streamers and showers of dust. Every step that Hooker took toward John Harris' table seemed to squelch up dust from the rug.

Hooker got to the table and stopped.

There was fallen John Harris. There was the box. Inside the box was the gun.

Hooker lifted the lid and looked. The purple silk

was dry and torn. The bullet box was set to one side. He ran his finger around the trigger guard and thought about what he was doing.

Gilbert. Shotgun.

He had heard his father's voice say that Gilbert was in trouble. He had heard Rosetta say they would hold a shotgun over Gilbert and that his father would do nothing. But something could be done.

If the gun was for Armageddon, a day of trouble, then Gilbert would need it now.

Gilbert would have the gun and be safe, and Hooker would have done it for him. Afterward, it could be returned, and it would be there at the other Armageddon, unless Armageddon came soon, in which case they would need the gun anyway, to take part in the killing.

Gilbert—they all—would be safe. They could help the Harrises, too. Mr. Harris was too old to fire the gun.

Hooker closed the lid and lifted the box up to his chest. He moved back toward the door, but as he passed by a low, wicker case of books, his eye was caught by a photograph, quite small, in a silver filigree frame. He had not seen it before.

Hooker stared, and the face in the frame stared back.

It was Rosetta.

Young.

The frame had a strange familiarity.

On the back porch, Alberta finished her song and stood up. Some robins flew around in a circle under the spray of the hose.

What time was it? Five thirty? Six?

Pretty nearly time for Teddy's dinner. Pretty nearly—the cocktail hour.

Alberta had avoided the gin bottle since morning and had been drinking orange juice instead. Inside, the kitchen table was littered with the pulpy remains of close to a dozen oranges, spread out over the oil cloth in the company of knives, spoons, and a large, hand-crank model squeezer. But now, she thought, a little bit of gin would perk the orange juice up.

She waddled down to the foot of the yard, splashing with her large spreading feet in their rubber shoes, in the small ponds and lakes that she had created over the last hours with the hose. The robins flew up onto the fence and into the trees to watch her.

"No, I ain't gonna keep watering," she said. "Don't you know 'bout this drought? They passed a hosing law. I gotta turn off this tap, or we'll all go to jail."

She turned off the tap, and the water thumped back along the hose.

"Anyhow," she said, drying her hands lightly against the weights of her breasts, "I ain't gonna stand here makin' rain till Doomsday. I got better things to do."

She turned and went into the house.

By now, Hooker was hiding in the cedar hedge, where he was forced to stay while an old man walked past, carrying his suit jacket and fanning himself with the evening newspaper.

Then, Hooker made a break for it and ran in the opposite direction, all the way to the corner. He cut through Cathy Moralt's side alley and banged through the wooden gate into the lane.

All the garbage cans were filled and ready to be picked up. They made a parade all the way, nearly four blocks off, to the rear of the Winslow house—where, Hooker could see, the procession ended or was broken, because Gilbert had not brought their own cans out yet.

The faraway gate swung open, and Iris came out into the lane. Hooker could see the white of her uniform and assumed that it was Iris and then was certain, once she had begun to call his name.

Where could he hide?

In the ditch.

Immediately, he flung himself across the lane and clambered down, with the box, into the weeds and grass. They were high enough to hide him if he lay down flat on the ground.

The sound of Iris' voice began its slow approach:

"Hooker! Hook—Hooker!"

Hooker made a small lookout through the weeds. Above him on the hydro and telephone wires, the starlings creaked and whistled like a bunch of old, unoiled gates, determined to draw attention to where he lay. At any other time, he thought, he would have fired the gun at them. He thought about Gilbert and Iris and their favorite words.

"Bugger off!" he growled from the ditch. "Bugger off!"

But the starlings did not move. They continued to whine and sing and rock in the wind, right above his head, like a message spoken down the wires.

He looked out at Iris. Beyond her, now, he saw that Gilbert had come through the gate with the bicycle and that he rode off, after a moment, toward the field and the wood. Iris was now quite close, within a block of where he lay.

"Hooker! Hooker! Hook!"

A few ants had begun to crawl along his arms and over his legs. He clenched his teeth. For once he wished that he had worn stockings that day, or even socks. The ants made a foray up to his trouser bottoms and then marched boldly inside his underwear. They sent patrols down the neck of his shirt; they drew up a parade on his shoulder blades. They chose sides and made a charge. He became a battleground. He was certain that he must yell out and give himself away.

Iris got to exactly where he was.

He heard her say, "Oh, to hell with it. I'll get back, and they'll turn him up on the phone."

She struck at a mosquito or a fly on her forearm, said "Ouch," and turned back.

After five minutes of agony, Hooker saw that she had reached the third block of distant houses. He stood up.

His plan was to get home and to hide the box in the stable. When Gilbert needed a gun, it would be there, and he could tell him that he had found it for him to use when he got into trouble. Then Gilbert would know that he had thought of him kindly. He would know that they could take sides together against people like Rosetta and their father and Mrs. Varley.

He ran down the lane, and it was almost dark.

He heard Gilbert arrive with the bicycle; he heard

him come through the gate, drop the bike by the porch, and go into the house.

He looked up at his mother's window. How much of this did she know about? And did it matter to her? Did she care?

He wished, standing in the stable and watching that one patch of light on the back wall of the house, that he could see her again. He tried to remember her untired face, but it was almost impossible. It had been so many months, almost years, since she had properly smiled at him and called him Hook.

He held the box in close against him.

She had read to him, touched him, brushed his hair, run her fingers down the small of his back; she'd held him in her arms. He could remember the smell of her perfume in the evenings. The room was always dark, with the orange shape of the open door and the lights beyond it, when she would appear, dressed in an evening gown and carrying a fur, and she would sit far onto his bed and tell him not to muss her hair. There were two bracelets she always wore, made of silver. One bore Gilbert's tooth marks and the other his own, and the story was that they had teethed on silver and would grow up to speak like kings. It was only a fairy tale, of course, but Hooker had once, quite recently, believed it. He had always loved to hold his own bracelet apart on her arm and then he would say, "I cut more marks than Gilbert did," and his mother would answer, "Yes, you did, Hook, because Gilbert was always shy," and they would rattle the bracelets, which made a soft, quiet sound. There was no third bracelet, however. It was as though his mother must have known somehow beforehand that this baby would die. She had not even gone to the store to buy one for him.

Suddenly, in the middle of this remembrance of the bracelets, the back door was flung open, and Gilbert, talking over his shoulder, came angrily into the yard.

"I wish to hell it was bloody legal to make some kids wear a ball and chain, that's all!" he said.

The screen door banged.

Hooker moved quickly.

There was just time to get to the loft. He flung himself at the ladder and clambered into the darkness, where he threw the box under some straw.

Gilbert came in and switched on the lights.

Hooker showed himself.

"Well! Where the Christ have you been?" his brother yelled.

"Don't yell," said Hooker. "Don't yell so loud."

"Then where have you been?"

"Asleep," said Hooker, rubbing his eyes against the glare of the light bulbs.

"Asleep! Where?"

The door from the porch came open again, and Iris, followed by Rosetta, stepped down into the yard.

"It's all right—he's here," said Gilbert. "Now, where the hell were you? Sleeping?"

Hooker blinked.

"Up here," he said. "In the straw."

"But we looked up there."

"Well, I can't help that. This's where I was."

"You're going to get a bloody good whipping for this. Nick is furious. He's even gone to the police station."

Hooker looked at his brother. He did not really

care. He had brought him the gun, and later on, Gilbert would understand. It was there, right now, in its box, safe until the shotgun came—under the straw in the old hayloft. At some future time Hooker would transfer it to the safety of his bedroom. Some night, perhaps in the dark the way it should be, he could explain it to Gilbert, and Gilbert would accept the weapon gratefully and realize that Hooker understood about trouble, understood about their father, and understood how difficult it was to be alone when people wanted to kill you.

Chapter Ten

August at last.

Clementine looked so fat now that Hooker wondered how she could move, but it did not seem to be a problem with her.

She had started her search for a nest. One day Gilbert found her in a bureau drawer with his underwear, and another day Iris discovered her lying in the cupboard where she kept the pots and pans; and her latest place was the third shelf of the hall closet. No one could figure out how she got there, because it was at least six feet off the ground.

From the back step, Hooker called, "Here, Clementine!"

It was a difficult name. She had been christened with it because of the song, which Hooker had always liked, but once the name had caught on, he realized that there was no suitable way of shortening it. He hated to call her "Clemmy," because one day he had, and Gilbert had said, "Here comes that girl with the clemmy hands," and Iris had laughed so long that Hooker had blushed. He did not call her "Clement," either, because that had brought on another of Gilbert's mystifying jokes—something about the

Pope—and "Tiny," especially once she was pregnant, was laughable even to Hooker.

So always, she received her full name, but Hooker had decided that her kittens would have simple names like Arthur, Penny, and David.

"Here Clement—ine! Clem—en—tine! Supper!"

The others all arrived on the porch, but Clementine had probably found a new nest and did not want to be disturbed. Hooker went back into the house.

They sat at the table together, not one of them speaking.

It was evening, and they were in the midst of eating a light meal—cheese soufflé and salad. Iris walked around the table, carrying the salad bowl one last time to make certain that everyone had what they needed. She poured a second glass of milk for Hooker, balancing the bowl over his head.

"Are we going to see Alberta?" he whispered.

"It ain't Thursday, hon."

"When is it Thursday, then?"

"Tomorrow."

Rosetta said, "Don't whisper, Hooker. That is rude."

"Yes'm."

"And you shouldn't encourage him, Iris. You know better than that."

"Yes, Miss Rose."

"Now, see that Mr. Winslow has the butter, please."

"Yes'm."

A silence descended, during which Iris tiptoed the full length of the table with the butter plate.

Hooker watched his brother, who sat across from

him.

Today, as had been true for a week now, Gilbert was quite drunk. He was picking at his food in such a way that it was clear he could not see it properly. A section of tomato, a piece of lettuce, and a two-inch square of soufflé lay on the mat beside his plate. Nobody had spoken to him, so far, during the entire meal.

Nicholas accepted the butter and waved Iris away. His eyes did not leave the circumference of his plate.

Hooker watched Gilbert.

Rosetta told him to EAT!

Upstairs, Jessica rang her brass bell.

"Go on, Iris," said Rosetta quietly. "We'll be all right."

Iris left them and went into the hall. They heard her climb the stairs. They could even hear her open Jessica's door. Hooker deciphered a few words. His mother wanted "some more coffee." Now Iris trudged all the way back and went straight on through to the kitchen.

Hooker had time to eat a piece of tomato and a whole green onion before she returned, coffeepot in hand.

She passed them importantly, on to the staircase and up through the door.... And back through the door— that soft click they all hated so, but at least, the key did not turn—and finally, she came down the stairs and into the dining room where Gilbert finally spoke:

"A nigger's work is never done, eh, Iris?"

The others looked at each other.

Iris said, "No, Mister Gil, you're right. A Negro's work is never done. Like the *work* of some other folks."

She continued, now, through to the kitchen, letting the door swing back and forth behind her, which punctuated the words like a T.V. cowboy fanning his six-gun.

Gilbert sat motionless over his food.

"Very clever," he muttered.

After a moment, Rosetta and Nicholas started to eat again. Hooker had finished, and he motioned for attention.

"No," said Rosetta. "You may not leave the table. Sit still until we have finished, too."

Suddenly Gilbert said, "Father?"

"Yes?" Nicholas said, looking up. His voice was blurred with food.

"Have you ever heard of a Mr. A. Parker?"

Hooker almost said out loud, "He has," but he stopped himself in time.

The color drained from Nicholas' face. It even seemed to drain from the tomatoes, the lettuce, and the soufflé on his plate. He flicked a glance at Rosetta, like a man opening a switchblade knife, and she responded by carefully laying down her implements, with a click, in the center of her plate.

Nicholas spoke as he might have if he had been asked, "Do you know Adolf Hitler?"

"Anthony Parker?" he said. "Yes."

"Railroad Parker is his real name."

"I've heard him called that, yes."

"The richest man alive," said Gilbert, sighing.

"I hardly think that's true," said Nicholas.

Rosetta stepped on the buzzer.

Hooker looked at father and thought about the gun.

Should he have told Gil? Were they going to kill him now? It was there in the stable.

Iris came back. She regarded Gilbert crookedly and said, "Yes?"

Rosetta said that they were ready for the sherbet, and immediately Iris propped open the door to the kitchen and began to clear away the dishes. Gilbert ignored her.

"Railroad Parker is so filthy rich, Father, that he actually has a villa in France and a winter place in Jamaica. Did you know that? He hardly really has to live here in Canada at all. 'Cept to count up his money...'cept to clip a few coupons...'cept to visit Bay Street..." He waved his hand conclusively.

"Well, lots of people are that rich, Gilbert."

"We aren't."

"Of course we aren't."

"We were, though. Once."

"Possibly. Before income taxes, in your grandfather's day. But that wasn't the same kind of money."

"Mother had money. Didn't she?"

"A little. Yes. What are you driving at?"

"Nothing. I'm not driving at anything. I'm just pointing out how much money there is—floating around. Naturally, I wouldn't want to stop it—fluctuating back and forth. But on the other hand, I wouldn't want to go poor."

Rosetta coughed.

Nicholas folded his napkin and immediately, nervously, opened it again and spread it across his legs like an apron.

"Gilbert, we are not poor at all. We're very well-off,

and you know that. You"—he could not refrain from this added sarcasm—"of all people should know that."

Gilbert smiled.

"You're not living here on your own money, for heaven's sake," Nicholas continued, without witnessing the smile.

"Whose money is it, then?"

Nicholas went red.

"Mine."

Rosetta could not help giving a sigh.

Nicholas said, "You have no personal inheritance, Gilbert."

Gilbert made a face of mock surprise and said, "Oh!"

"Gilbert!"

It was Rosetta, but Nicholas said, "Don't," and she subsided.

Gilbert winked—or tried to wink—at Hooker.

"Are you asking about an inheritance?" Nicholas asked, still speaking quietly.

Gilbert set down his fork at last and let Iris take away his plate of unfinished food. He drew in a breath.

"No," he said diffidently. "No. No. Not exactly."

"Don't you feel well-provided for, then? What is it?"

"For God's sake, Nicholas..." Rosetta could not contain herself any longer. Pushing her chair back, she inadvertently shook the table.

Gilbert laughed. "A good example, eh, Rose? Sort of perfect. Almost."

"What do you mean?" said Nicholas, thinking wildly that perhaps his sister and his son were conspiring against him together. "What do you mean?

Example of what?" Inside, his temper and his fear rose, like tides, together.

"Blackmail," said Gilbert. "Of course."

Iris stopped dead in her tracks.

Hooker, tennis-watching, turned now to his father, whose expression was one of uncertainty.

"I take it," Nicholas said—and the continued quiet of his tone made Hooker wonder at his patience—"that you mean to imply that *you* are blackmailing *me*."

"Take it any way you like," said Gilbert, closing his mouth tight against a belch.

Nicholas took a deep draft of consideration from the atmosphere of the room.

"But I don't have to keep you here, and I don't have to give you any *more* money," he said finally.

Rosetta placed one hand against her forehead and watched. Her mouth was still and hard; her eyes were honed and sharpened like a pair of knives.

"I think you're wrong about that," said Gilbert. "Because—"

"You do?"

"Yes. I do."

All of a sudden, Nicholas caught sight of Iris.

"Iris. Please. Go and get the dessert. Take that damned salad out of here," he said. His tone of voice had still not changed.

Iris went away with the salad bowl.

Gilbert took out his cigarettes and lighted one nervously while Nicholas watched him.

"But under the terms by which, apparently, you continue to keep me here, *I* think you must go on paying me. Yes," Gilbert said, picking up the conversation as though a bell had rung for the end of the intermission.

Hooker gripped his chair seat with both hands, prepared to be told to leave.

But the order never came. Instead, Iris returned with a tray of sherbet glasses and served them, one by one, very quickly, all around the table. The atmosphere was just exactly as it had been when Hooker's mother was first ill—when they did not know what she might say and do next.

"Well," said Nicholas, "get on with it. I might as well hear what you have to say."

"I've said it," said Gilbert. "Didn't you hear me?"

Nicholas looked genuinely puzzled.

"No. What was it?" he asked. "I don't think I understood."

Gilbert sat back in his chair, smoking very carefully, speaking very quietly.

"It's Mr. Parker," he said. "Mr. Railroad Parker— and his family."

Chapter 11

It was such a short answer that Nicholas was not prepared for it. He seemed dumbfounded and just sat there, staring almost vacantly at the words "and family," where they hung, like a broken pendulum, between himself and his son.

"Mr. Parker's family?"

"Yes."

Rosetta closed her eyes.

"You didn't go to see him—did you, Father."

It was not a question.

"But I don't know him..." Nicholas started to say, "...that well," he concluded. And then, very delicately, "I have no reason, anyway, to go and see him."

"All right. You don't know him. But you do know me," said Gilbert.

Hooker thought, "He's over being drunk. He's not drunk anymore."

Nicholas, equally scrutinized by Rosetta, gave a long, hard look at Gilbert. He moved his jaw from side to side while his face began to redden. The words "fear" and "care" seemed to be written in either eye.

"However well I may know you, Gilbert," he said, "doesn't help me in knowing what the hell you're talking about. I simply don't know what you're talking about, and I think this conversation had better end. You're drunk, and—"

Immediately Gilbert heard the word "drunk," he struck his fist against the table. The effect of this was the same as it would have been had he struck Nicholas on the mouth.

Gilbert said, "Am I supposed to have knocked up Janice Parker or not, Father? Did I—or didn't I?"

He stood up.

Nicholas, having received the effects of a physical blow, let all his words fall away with his hands, which collapsed, knocking aside a glass of water onto the table.

It was an earthquake, Hooker thought. The room was falling over.

"But…" Nicholas tried to begin, "I didn't really think…"

"Yes, you did! Yes, you did!"

"I didn't *know*…"

"Then why didn't you come to me?" Gilbert's voice rose. "Why didn't you come and ask me?"

They waited.

"Aren't you ever going to say no—or try to stop me? Why don't you get off your goddamned ass?"

Silence.

"Beat the bloody shit out of me?"

Gilbert was crying with rage, like a child. Like a friend, Hooker thought, his own age.

"What's wrong? What is wrong? Aren't you my father? I'd like to know what kind of fucking father *you* had. What kind of father was that bloody photograph in the other room? He must've thought he had a bunch of goddamn saints on his hands, what with perfect you and perfect Pat and perfect sweet Rosetta." He turned on his father with one last phrase: "Or did he just have contempt for you, the way you have for me—and *all* your children, dead or alive?"

Nicholas, Rosetta, Iris, and Hooker all stared. It was a miracle of words. Gilbert, like God, had spoken. They watched him and waited for more.

Gilbert, pushing over his chair so that it fell against the window, left the room. His departure was as absolute as the end of a sentence to which there was no reply. They were speechless.

They sat still in their places just for a moment, and then Rosetta, Iris, and Hooker went away into the body of the house, leaving Nicholas alone in the dining room, which became a cavern, holding him underground. And, like a cavern too, it held the late words of argument up for him to hear—visible echoes, which he stared at vacantly until his mind shifted, made room, and let them in.

Nicholas went away then, out of the house and into his late father's stable.

Nicholas opened the door of Gilbert's Jaguar and got in.

Where did Gilbert go in this expensive, sporty little car? To the Parkers'? To other parties, with other girls? Girls? Nicholas had never met and did not even know of them. He must have friends. He must have "hangouts"—places where he met people. Where did he drink, for instance, aside from the times he drank locked up in the library?

Nicholas thought he would never know. How could you know, unless you asked? And how could you ask unless you were on speaking terms?

It was true. He did not speak with his wife, and now he did not speak with his children. Only with his sister—that "sweet child," as Gilbert called her. They talked, and she decided things.

At business he was a stranger to himself. He functioned, he did things—bought and sold stocks and told his employees what to do—but these were automatic gestures in deference to the facts of life. To the edict that in society you must do something to belong. To the edict of continuity, generation to generation. His work needed none of his personality, and now neither did his family. He felt lonely. He sat there, in Gilbert's car, trying to remember his own youth, his own car, his own drinking, and his own girls. But they were as vague in his mind and as remote as Gilbert's own anonymous life. Perhaps there had been no girls. He could not remember.

He thought of his wife. Jessica. Once he had courted her, calling in a car just as sporty and right as this—the old McLaughlin—and they had driven to Lake Simcoe, and they had made a kind of love where there were woods and an old cottage, and Jessie had said...Jessie said...

Was it possible? He could not remember.

Jessie had said, "You..."

But the words would not come to him. They were gone. It was over. Like his children, those past parts of his own life were dead or buried, one way or another, forever.

He looked around him, remembering his father's horses, perfectly, by name: "Tall Boy...Gadabout... Careless Mary..." And remembering his father, he could see the man who had talked to him so quietly, so easily, such a long time ago. He had had such a peaceful tone of voice...his eyes were so...his hands...were so...what he was was so...so very...very strong. And alive.

Nicholas wept.

In the house, the atmosphere was so tense that they had forgotten to turn on the lights.

Rosetta, in her office, sat in a deep gloom, almost utterly dark, and the kitchen was only lighted with sunset. While upstairs Jessica's bedroom glowed with the glassy reflections of that same sun, balanced in its flames eight individual times in the panes of an open window.

They could all hear the same robins and even the muted traffic from the far-distant city. Even Nicholas, sitting out in the stable, could hear, but he did not listen.

Now, Iris and Hooker and Rosetta waited.

Rosetta sat very still. She seemed to listen. And then a noise came.

The library door opened.

Gilbert came into the hall.

He said, "Mother!"

Rosetta winced and sat forward, pressing her diaphragm in against the edge of her desk.

Iris, rocking back and forth with Hooker huddled

in her lap, stopped short. Hooker made a move.

"Wait," said Iris.

"MOTHER?"

Gilbert's voice had thickened with the extra whiskey. To the listeners, he sounded like someone calling from under water.

They heard him move.

Hooker sat straight up.

"Now, wait," said Iris softly. "We will wait for Miss Rose to go first."

They listened again.

"Are you going to come down?" said Gilbert. "Or am I going to come up?"

There was no answer, but in her bed, setting aside a book she had ceased to read when the sunlight had begun to fail, Jessica heard him and turned her face toward the door.

"You aren't really sick, you know," Gilbert called out. "And we all know that."

Silence.

"What are you going to do about it?"

No answer.

"Mother?"

Rosetta stood up and went to the door of the office. But went no further.

"No one's going to hurt you, Mother. If you come down, we'll just sit and talk like we used to, in the living room."

Jessica was obviously listening. Her bed made a creaking sound. Perhaps she was sitting up, rearranging her covers.

"I want to talk to you."

Rosetta placed a hand on her cheek.

They could all hear him move farther into the hall, probably right to the foot of the stairs.

"I tried to talk to Father, but he won't listen."

Iris coughed.

"There's nobody here but me," said Gilbert.

Jessica's feet made a gentle noise against the floor. There was a further sound, suggesting that she was fumbling for her slippers.

"Mama! I have got to talk to you!"

In the bedroom, something fell.

"Mom?"

Instantly, Rosetta came through the office door, and Iris, dumping Hooker, made for the hallway. Gilbert heard Iris, and he saw Rosetta with her hands outstretched. He moved.

When he got to Jessica's door, she was already fumbling with the key, but he was through and on the inside before she could turn it in its lock.

"Get away from me!" she said. "Get away!"

Gilbert locked the door.

Rosetta and Iris stood on the stairs.

"Wait a minute," said Rosetta. "If we wait a minute, it could be all right."

"He's awful drunk...." said Iris.

"We'll wait," said Rosetta.

"What for?" said Iris. "Murder?"

"He only wants to talk to her, Iris. Now, go back to the kitchen. Look after Hooker."

Iris moved off down the hall.

"Talk!" she said. "Hah!"

"You be ready," said Rosetta, "and when I call, you

damn well come."

"Yes'm."

Iris returned to the kitchen.

In the hallway, Rosetta turned on the lights. With a final look at Jessica's door, she went back into her office and sat down. She switched on one lamp there, on her desk. Outside, she could just see to the stable doors, open, and the shape of her brother's head and shoulders, where he sat utterly still in Gilbert's car.

Iris said, "Now, let's suppose that sometimes it's good for people to yell a little at each other. Eh, Hook? Sometimes, like this house, we'll suppose that it gets so quiet that you can't tell what anybody feels any-more. Now, Gilbert is drunk, but he is not going to hurt your mom. He would never hurt anybody."

Hooker thought about that. "He said he could kill my cats."

"That's just a way of talking, hon. Only something he says."

"Why didn't Rosetta stop him?"

"Well, A—she's not big enough to stop him, an' B—I think she's got some idea about how this'll be good for Gilbert. An', like I said, she could be right. Maybe he just needs to get something out of his system."

"But," she added to herself, "I don't think so."

She rocked back and forth, with Hooker held on her lap. It was like old times.

"Your knees are hard," said Hooker, remembering.

"Tough," said Iris. "I ain't complainin' 'bout your behind, am I?"

"No."

"Then be quiet and sit still."

Hooker subsided.

At last he said, "Remember when we used to do this?"

"I sure do. Just as if it was yest'day."

"What's going to happen?" said Hooker.

"Nothin's gonna happen. We're gonna be all right."

A crash was heard upstairs.

Iris listened for Rosetta. But she did not come from her office or call.

"This is like some sort of an air raid," said Iris.

"Or like Armageddon," said Hooker.

From upstairs, they could almost distinguish a few raucous words.

"...but he wouldn't listen—he would not listen...."

Iris said, "Talkin' 'bout your father."

Hooker said, "Something will happen—it will. It will happen."

"What, honey? What will?"

"I don't know," said Hooker. "But it will. Something will."

They sat still. Iris ruminated, looking out the window.

"Oh, if I could only figure out your father, I'd have an awful big answer," she muttered, and overhead, they heard Jessica say, "Dead! Dead! Dead!"

Hooker pressed in, and uniform buttons scratched against his ear.

"She meant the baby," he said. "She says it's dead."

They waited. At their feet, the cats, all but Clementine, rose and turned and lay down again, with staring eyes.

"That baby has been dead months, now," said Iris.

Rosetta, turning from the view of Nicholas in the car, sat far back into her office chair and closed her eyes. She heard the crash upstairs and the voices, but she could not gain the moral momentum to intervene.

Years, and ancestors, leaned in against her.

She thought, "Maybe we should all die. Maybe we should all just be satisfied to die."

Then she opened her eyes and searched for John Harris. Her gaze found a small silver frame, the twin of the one that Hooker had seen in the Harrises' living room, surrounding her old ability to smile.

"Family," she said to John Harris. "It's come to be the worst word I know, now."

John Harris smiled.

Jessica said, "Dead...dead...dead..." and Rosetta winced with the free side of her face.

She looked out the window at Nicholas.

She thought, "I have been left without any men to take care of me."

Upstairs Gilbert said, "It isn't true. That is not true."

Rosetta listened to him. He was walking up and down.

"Don't you know what's happening in this house?"

Rosetta could not make out the reply. She got out of her chair.

Jessica screamed. She began to ring her bell.

Rosetta went into the hall.

"Iris!"

Iris appeared at once.

"He is not talking," said Rosetta. "He is just yelling

at her."

"Listen, shouldn't we get Mr. Winslow? Shouldn't I go out and get him?" said Iris.

"We must excuse Mr. Winslow from this," said Rosetta.

"But Miss Rose—" Iris was astounded. The word "excuse"…

Rosetta looked at her.

"Don't you understand *anything*?" Rosetta hissed.

Iris said, "I only understan' we gotta do something. That's all. An' Mr. Winslow—"

"Well, if you can get Gilbert out of there, then go on up."

Iris swallowed.

"I still say Mr. Winslow…" she muttered. But she did not finish. Clear as a bell they heard Jessica raising her voice, word by word, and the sound of it made them freeze in their tracks.

"I will not…" they heard her say, "…go on. I will not go…on…giving…birth…to you…and to Hooker …and to that…god…damned…baby…day…after… bloody… day…for the rest of my LIFE! Can't I ever be free of that?"

Iris moved.

"The mere idea that you were ever—inside of me…" Jessica's voice had gone dead. "I can't bear you… Don't you—won't somebody understand that? I hate you!"

By now Iris was at the door.

"Gil," she said. "Gilbert?"

"Open the door," said Jessica. "Open the door."

The key was turned.

Hooker, with his cats, was now standing by the green folds of the living-room drapes and could just make out the edge of Gilbert's shirted shoulder and his head. And then Iris passed in and closed the door.

"Get out of here," she said.

"I only wanted to speak to her," said Gilbert.

Jessica was weeping.

"That you have done," said Iris. "Now get out of here."

"But she's my mother," said Gilbert quietly.

Rosetta held onto the newel post.

"Listen," said Iris, "I said *get the hell* out of here."

Silence.

"And you listen—you black fart—don't talk to me like that..."

Iris snapped, "Get out!"

The door opened, and this was followed by Gil's ejection into the hall.

Iris slammed the door.

Gilbert looked at it and then yelled, "You and that supposed—mother figure—in there can shut every fucking door from here to Jesus Christ, but you'll never get rid of this family. We're all here to stay—you hear me!"

He struck the door once with his fist. And then, as he turned away, he found that his shirt, somehow, was caught in the doorjamb. He made a noise that Hooker had never heard a human being make before that moment. It was an animal noise—of pain—just the sort of noise that the squirrel had made before it had died.

And suddenly Nicholas was there, at last.

Hooker looked at his father and bit one of his

cuticles until it bled.

Gilbert came away from the door with a painful wrenching of his wrists, twisting in a circular, awkward lurch. And with him, as though from a distance, a flurry of scattered, unheard-of adjectives fell upon the ears below like snow that is gone before it has touched the ground.

Now, as those below him waited, the whole of this enormous movement brought him all at once in collision with the stare of the cats.

Downstairs, Rosetta, Nicholas, and Hooker strained up, toward the sounds.

Hooker stepped forward, thinking of the gun.

Gilbert's mouth opened and closed. He heaved. Liquid vomit—nothing but beer and wine—belched out of him onto the rug at the top of the stairs....

The bedroom door opened, quietly this time, and the head and shoulders of Iris made a foray into the upper hallway.

"What's that noise?" she said. "I heard someone throw up."

"It's nothing," Gil said flatly. "Go on back in."

Iris looked darkly at Gil, withdrew from the hall without comment, and closed the door.

Gil rested his whole body upon his hands, placing his weight carefully, as someone in a balancing act would do, against the upper banister.

"What time is it?" he asked.

Idiotically, they all but Hooker looked at their watches, but no one spoke.

"Can I get something to eat?" said Gil. His eyes were quite wide open but still uncleared and stare-y.

Nicholas looked up.

"Sick, for Jesus' sake..." he said, making an unful-filled gesture of impotent repulsion with his hands.

Gilbert's feet were entangled in each other. He shuf-fled them.

"I'm hungry," he said. "I haven't been hungry in days."

Nicholas walked away, then, into the living room.

Rosetta watched him go. She saw that he was only turning on the lamps. Her gaze slid away and up to where Gil stood.

Hooker sat down on the bottom step and was still, just very still, waiting for the next thing to happen—whatever it would be.

Rosetta walked away down the dark part of the hallway, toward the kitchen.

Gil was staring down at the lower hall, his eyes dancing in and out of focus. Hooker began to run his fingers over the carpeting on the stairs, lifting away traces of cat hair. He did this the way other people doodle.

Presently Rosetta returned, wearing rubber gloves, wide and gaping at the cuff, and carrying a box and a few rags.

She went up the stairs.

"Stand away," she said to Gilbert.

Gil, without looking at her, sidled along the banis-ter like a large bird—like a vulture, because his shoul-ders were rounded over.

"Further," said Rosetta.

Then he shifted further and watched what she was doing.

"What's that?" he said.

"You were sick," replied Rosetta.

Gil looked over the rail at Hooker. His view of him now was only of the top of his head and part of the curve of his shoulders. "I fwowed up," he baby-talked. And promptly threw up again into the hall below.

Hooker's cats ran in all directions.

"Oh, don't," someone said. "Don't, Gil! Don't anymore!"

Nicholas appeared in the living-room doorway below. He still had his handkerchief in his hands.

"Shall I call the doctor," he said, "again?"

He spoke the words as a very bad actor might have spoken them.

They had never seen Gil so drunk. He had the look of a man who was about to have an epileptic attack—childishly vague and viciously self-protective. He merely stood there, staring at their faces, each without focus.

And then he said, "I'm going to laugh."

There was a long moment.

Rosetta and Nicholas and Hooker watched him carefully until finally he did.

Later that night, Gilbert drove off in the red Jaguar and drank beer in one of the beer parlors on the outskirts of town.

At one point he went into the washroom, locked himself in one of the cabinets, and wept, privately, for ten minutes. Then he dried his face with toilet paper and flushed the toilet, the latter lest anyone should think he had not used the cabinet for legitimate reasons. He was about to leave when he saw written, along with the messages of perversion and loneliness on the wall, the words JESUS SAVES.

He stared. And smiled.

Neatly, and with deliberate sobriety, he appended the words AND GOD SPENDS alongside, and went back to the beer parlor and his beer, banging all the intervening doors behind him.

When he got home that night, he turned the Jaguar into the driveway without reducing speed. There was a red skunk in his path. He ran it down and killed it, because he had never seen a red skunk before and he thought, with that exquisite logic that comes with drunkenness, "No one will believe me unless I kill it and show them."

Of course, there is no such thing as a red skunk.

It was Clementine.

Chapter Twelve

Just after sunrise the next morning, Hooker put Clementine in a large box and put the box itself on his chipped red wagon. He started off from the back of the house, toward the field.

The sun was low but very hot.

Everything was perfectly still. Hooker and the wagon moved off, while his mother and Iris looked on from different windows.

Iris stood at the kitchen window. Jessie, who had been awake all night, peered through the gauze of her curtains, upstairs.

Hooker wore his straw hat, the one with the ribbons. To the onlookers, his back seemed exceptionally straight this morning, and there as a sweat patch, like a stripe, down the center of his shirt. He wore his short pants, no socks as usual, and running shoes. His legs were gold in color and very strong.

He took a measured step, singing the song he had learned from Iris:

"Frankie and Johnnie were lovers!
Oh, lordy, how they could love...."

Jessica from her window watched the ribbons and saw how very straight they fell from the brim of the hat, almost to his waist.

Iris idled over the stirring of some johnnycake batter.

At last, even the sound of the song was gone, and the two women relaxed.

Hooker came off the lane to the low, indefinite crest of the first hill and saw the woods.

"We must go through that dark," he thought, "with all the birds asleep."

And aloud:

> "Frankie went down to the pawn shop,
>   She bought herself a little forty-four...."

The hill fell down away from him, and the wagon clattered loudly over the grass and the loose carth.

> "Root-a-toot, three times she shot,
>   Right through that hardwood floor...."

The path was too narrow for the axle, and so the wheels spanned the ridges on either side.

Hooker looked back at Clementine. The lid from her box was completely gone, some place. But he did not stop.

In the patchy dark of the trees he sang, with harrowed concentration, about Frankie and her lover:

> "Oh, bring on your rubber-tired hearses,
>   Oh, bring on your rubber-tired hacks.

They're takin' your man to the graveyard,
And they ain't goin' to bring him back...."

The trees began to stand apart, and there came much more sunlight now than dark. Hooker stopped singing.

There was a pause, it seemed, in the landscape.

"Now, Clementine," he said, and said it aloud, which made a few birds go up from the grass. They flew from there to the distant trees.

Hooker drew the mean, red wreck with its corpse into the sunlight.

The field, as though planned, was quiet.

Hooker paused and breathed in.

He removed his straw hat, looped the ribbons carefully out of the breeze, and laid it on the wagon. He stepped to the grave site and hunkered down.

The early sun was already broiling hot, and Hooker felt wet all over. He drew some grass stems rhythmically through the palm of his hand. He turned his head to one side and laid it close against his bare knee, and this way he could see through the grass to the trees and to the sky faraway. A blue jay was idling in the air, about to drop back to shelter. It paused, in slow motion, to look across toward this place.

The silence was long and still.

Gradually Hooker looked away and tried to focus on the earth itself. He cleaned a bit of it just in front of him by removing stones and grass and making a small pile of refuse.

Automatically he watched to see the dragonflies, and seeing them, he made a sound of recognition.

There seemed to be hundreds of them, flying up out of the grass.

Some ants made a weaving motion across the dirt.

Hooker went away and got the burial spoon.

The earth was dry on top and moist further down. A deep, rich smell came up as he dug, a smell of roots and decay and old, round stones. Worms fled from the edge of the spoon as it flashed in and out of the ground, gleaming and wet. The ants tramped on, struggling over the loose, newly dug soil, their direction without change.

Everything was in motion.

The mound of earth grew upon itself.

Hooker removed his shirt. He became dirty.

His eyes glassed over and burned a little with salt. He drew his wrist across his face and went on working.

At last it was done, and he went back for Clementine.

The animal felt strangely warm in his hands, and her red, red coat did not look dead yet. Hooker rocked her, just for a moment, and held her close against his skin. When he had put her down, he stood very straight above her and looked at the red against the earth.

"Good little girl. Good Clementine," he said.

He thought of her kittens. He did not even know how many there would have been.

The breeze lingered over the listless tail, fingering her coat and shifting the shapes of the white-tipped tags of fur, where there were snags he had not brushed and hair-enclosed burrs from the last time they had hunted through the undergrowth, probably here, in the field.

Hooker sank down and sat back on his heels. He

dangled the spoon from his fingers. Finally, he lifted Clementine into the grave and just stared at her.

He hummed the tune, once through, and then stopped.

All over the fidd, the dragonflies caught at the grass and blew in the breeze, with gestures of resistance, to and fro. Hooker had to squint to see them. He began to place the earth on top of Clementine.

On the way home through the woods, Hooker opened his ears, and the noises everywhere were suddenly wonderful to hear. With a rush, like fast water, came the loud and perfected outcry of all living things, spilling out in motion —wings and legs and tails and eyes—flashing up to make an open way for his running and for the crazy dragging of the wagon after him, red, through the trees, emptied of its burden, thrashing up the old dust and shaking out the sparrows like leaves, into a windy air.

Seen from the hills, the wood, all pale, was lifted from its sleep by the explosion of these urgent wings, and it rang with the sound of Hooker running, in a hunt without a prey.

Chapter Thirteen

The elm trees were beginning to be tipped with brown curls in the drought. Hooker sat on the porch roof and looked at them. When would it rain?

Around him, on the shingle roof, his three remaining cats stretched in the sun. They did not seem to know that Clementine was dead.

Hooker thought, however, that it could be that the cats might know something that he did not know. They might even know that being dead is something different from what we think it is. Maybe they even see each other dead, or something....

He thought about it, sitting very still, watching Little Bones.

She was so quiet and so peaceful that he thought, "Nothing can happen to her." And yet, once now, a cat had died.

Hooker could see down into the dust of the yard, and he could see the stable, painted red, and beyond that, into the alley over the yard fence. He could see along the alley, too, and on up to the gentle hill, where he had been before breakfast, and almost into the woods.

Everywhere there was the still, warm smell of summer flowers, laced with the sour aroma of grass smoke. Some-one, faraway, was burning a field to prevent the woods from catching fire. At first, when Hooker had been told about this, it had not made sense to him. It seemed so peculiar to destroy one perfectly good thing in place of another. As though it mattered less that grass should burn than trees.

Looking up, Hooker watched some birds—some starlings and a white wheel of pigeons as they passed over the sky.

Usually, this was such a good time of year, he thought. Then he thought of Markham College and how that had been ruined for him now.

The whole summer was ruined. Everything was ruined. Yesterday had finally ruined it all. Iris would have said to grin and bear it, but he could not do that.

Tomorrow was to have been the very best day of all.

The Midsummer Ball was to take place then at his father's country club, and this year, for the first time—because of his impending entrance to an "adult" school—Hooker was to be allowed to attend. He would be there right through the dance and everything.

But it was ruined. It was all ruined. His family would not speak to one another. His cat was dead. He would never see the kittens being born. They were dead. It was so confusing. Nicholas had left for the city without saying good-bye even to Rosetta, and Iris had grumped around the kitchen all morning. Rosetta was checking everyone's clothes for the party, and the house smelled of mothballs and dust. Gilbert was in the library and had been there all night long. Hooker wondered if he even knew that he had run over and killed Clementine. Certainly, if he did know, he had forgotten. No one had said a word about it all morning, except Iris, who had said, "D'ja get that done then, honey?" when he had come back from the burial. But no one seemed to have really taken it in.

He lay back. The gun—what use now was the gun? He had transferred it to his own room, despairing of Gilbert's need for it. He felt—although he did not, of course, know so—like a lover who has bought a ring for a girl who announces her engagement to someone else.

The trees were woven together above him like a puzzle, so he closed his eyes. The gun was his now, he thought. And then it was that it happened.

Seemingly from a great distance he began to hear a noise.

At first he thought that it was just someone sawing wood, but since the sound grew in volume, he concluded that it must be something else, something that was moving toward him where he lay.

It took on a slightly mechanical tone.

"It's a motorcycle," he said out loud.

But it was not a motorcycle.

Hooker tightened his eyelids.

Now it sounded like a beehive.

But where was there a beehive? Only away out where Mr. MacArthur, the bee man, lived, and that was far too faraway for him to hear it from this house.

He opened his eyes and looked at the sky. But there was nothing there except the branches and the birds.

Gradually he realized that the noise had stopped.

Some crows were retreating from the town, and they headed, over him, for the woods. He watched the tattered battleflags of their wings and heard their voices, like distant laughter. He wondered whom they had warred against, and where. They came over like that nearly every day now, and probably they chose different places, where they raided the nests of the town's sparrows and starlings, robins and grackles. A starling lived in the stable roof. Slowly, even the noise of the crows subsided.

What was that other noise?

He closed his eyes again.

"It is bees," he thought. "Or something with long wings, big enough to buzz—and there are hundreds of them...."

"Hooker!"

He sat up.

It was Iris.

"Milk time—an' you can eat more johnnycake, if you want it."

He did not answer.

She stood right below him on the step.

"Hooker!"

"Yes," he said quietly.

Iris jumped.

"Don't go and dream up there, honey. You'll get sunstroke and go in a coma. C'mon down now and have your milk."

Hooker chicken-walked to the edge of the roof and jumped.

"Someday, you'll have broken ankles and broken wrists and a broken neck, if you don't watch it," said

Iris, holding the door open for him.

"Or a broken bum," said Hooker.

"Now, you stop that," said Iris.

"Everybody else swears around here. Even you."

"That is not swearing—that is plain and simple dirty. Wash your hands and sit down."

The milk and the johnnycake sat neatly on the kitchen table. Hooker ran the water, and having flicked his fingers at it, he sat down.

"You didn't dry."

"Yes, I did."

Iris was too tired to press the matter further.

"Just don't bounce round in your chair, 'cause I got a lemon cake in the oven."

Hooker fidgeted.

"Can I have coffee?"

"No."

"Can I have more milk, then?"

"You ain't finished that yet."

He drank the whole glassful in one continuous gulp. Iris sighed. "Bottle's in the fridge," she said.

Hooker went across the room and got out the milk.

"Will you please pour it in your glass? Honest to God, your mother would really wonder how I brung you up!"

Hooker poured another full glass of milk and, leaving the bottle on the table, sat down.

There was silence.

Iris, who was drinking coffee, looked from the window.

"Looks like all the heat in hell is outside there," she said. "Look't it. Shimmers like on a lake, don't it?"

Hooker did not speak. He concentrated on the sounds that seemed, now, to be emanating from the corners of the room.

Iris, misinterpreting his silence, said, "You know, down in Carter's Bridge, I had all kinds of cats, once, too. White ones, black ones, gray... Everybody had kids and cats. By the zillion. Kids and cats."

She placed the yellowed crinkles of her hands on the table top and considered the state of her ragged nails. She looked askance at Hooker.

His silent listening widened and became obstinate.

"You know," she said, "dying happens every day, Hook. Lookit your cats and them birds."

She reneged on that subject and returned to her own cats.

"Most kids have cats, I guess—or a dog or something. There is always something when you're young. I guess it's true I had maybe eighteen cats in all, all told," she said. "Starting with one I called Maxine. I always found Maxine a pretty name for a cat—like it's sort of the way a cat really is. Max—eeeen," she laughed.

She drank some coffee.

"Albert...Violet...Delbert...George... I forget why I called him that, George—more'n likely I had a beau named George, or it was someone I liked, anyway. Bruce...Jeanette...Purlie...Grace...Raina...Daisy... That makes"—she counted over the names, tapping them out with her fingers—"eleven. Well, maybe not eighteen, but there's eleven that I remember, all quite clearly. And they all had to go, and they all had to die, one way or another."

She mused over the thought of it.

Hooker had barely heard all this and cheated some coffee into his glass of milk. Iris noticed but did not say so.

"I have always respected the laws of give and take," she said formally. "They can't be argued with—they're always there. In life. Like Clementine. That's one of the first things to learn. If you can't learn the facts, you might as well be done."

Hooker said very quietly, "I didn't say I even missed her."

Iris blinked heavily. "No, honey."

"Everybody has got to die."

"That's right. The baby and the cats and me an' you."

"It was just an accidental death—like in the papers."

"Right."

She slid a few vagrant crumbs of breakfast cake across the table top toward the edge—and looked at him.

"What's really in your mind of minds?" she said. "Somethin's there."

Hooker thought. "I don't know."

And then, in a moment, he said, "I just don't like the way everybody always walks away from things. Everything."

Iris looked at him.

"Now, honey. They don't, really."

"They do. They walk off, all the time. Like they walked off on Gilbert. Like Gil walked off on me. On Clementine, too."

"It's just part of them being old. That's all."

"You're old."

"Anh!"

"You are!"

"I'm another person. Not like that."

"Why don't you walk off, then?"

"I do."

"Well, I've never seen it."

"You've never been there."

That was a mystery. He felt unprivileged.

"What do you mean?"

"Part of my private life. Not to do with you. Back at the Bridge."

"How old are you?" he asked suddenly.

"I'm not going to tell you, Hookie," Iris laughed. "You're always askin' me that, ever since you were able to see me. An' that's rude. I'm a woman, Hook—you can't ask me that."

She was silent.

"Why don't you phone somebody?" she asked, a moment later.

"Who? Why? Who?"

Iris stood up and went to the oven.

"Someone you can play with."

"I'd leave town before I'd play with anyone," said Hooker.

"Go on the lawn and play croquet, then, by yourself."

"No."

"All right, then, if you ain't got something to do, you can do something for me. You can go to the store. I need some paper napkins."

"Napkins?"

"Blue ones. Here." She delved into her purse for money.

"Why can't Harry bring them?"

"Because. Now go on. Be a good boy."

She turned her back on him.

Little Bones made an entrance through the push-open door. She meowed.

Hooker caught her in his arms, but she pushed away, scratching him on the chest with her back claws.

He bled and touched it with his fingers.

Iris paid little attention. It happened all the time. She tossed him a wet cloth, barely turning to look at him.

"A good smack is the answer to that," she mumbled. "Those damn cats..."

Hooker wiped off his skin. "Iris?"

She was back by the stove, bending in toward the open oven, whence heat came over the room in a rush with the smell of spices and lemons.

"Haven't you gone yet?"

"What was it Gil did say to her?"

Iris shrugged as though he had asked her almost any trivial question.

"A few things," she said. "Just a few things."

"How come you all yelled at each other?"

Iris was silent.

"Well, we all heard you," said Hooker.

She straightened.

Finally she said, "Gilbert is in some grown-up trouble, that's all."

Hooker waited. Would she mention the shotgun?

"Your mother didn't know that. And he wanted to explain."

Iris stretched, lifting the cake, looking at it against the light from the window. She walked toward the table to put it down. She gave a very long sigh.

"You know how sick your mama is, don't you?"

"Sure."

"Can you understand it, then, if I tell you that a part of that sickness is she doesn't always want to remember that Gil is her son? Like you are. Sometimes she don't remember that you are, either, which is why you never see her. In a way, you could say she's fed up with being part of the family. But it's only a sickness. It's not a real feeling or something she really wants to give up. It's simply—well, part of being sick. It's as simple as that."

"Why?"

"Why what?"

"Why is she fed up with being part of the family. She's my mother."

"Because being a mother is—I dunno—pain, to her, and trouble."

Iris turned to find a knife.

"Who said she had to be my mother anyway, if she hates it so much?"

"Your dad and your mom agreed on it together."

"When?"

"Before you were born, of course."

"What'd they do? Talk about it? Sit down and talk about it?"

"Yes."

"Then why can't they talk it over again?"

"They did. And so your mom was a mom again, but that baby died, and—"

"I don't mean that—I mean, be *my* mother. And Gilbert's."

Iris tasted some crumbs and said, "Now listen. If I could explain it to you, I would. But I can't explain it any more than that. I can only give you a few ideas, and that's all. Your mom is sick. Your dad and your mom don't want to sit down and talk it over. It's made you unhappy. It's made Gil unhappy, your Aunt Rose an' me unhappy, too. That is really all I know."

She had lost patience.

Hooker knew it.

"Then what are we going to do?" he said, staring at her.

"You're gonna go and get the napkins, that's what you're gonna do."

"I don't mean that."

"Listen, I'll whale you if you don't stop this!"

"Then why don't you whale Gil because he killed my cat?"

"Because he was stoned, that's why. Because you never hit somebody who's drunk. Or sick..." she began to say.

Hooker went white, and his eyes grew narrow.

"Like crazy people get forgiven? Nutty people? Is that it?"

Iris stared at him.

"Hooker!"

"Does it mean, if I get crazy, then I can do anything, too? Anything? Is that what it means? I think so...."

He turned and walked out of the room.

For the first time, Iris thought, she had heard the adult in Hooker—the sort of adult you would accuse of being childish.

"Jesus! What has someone said?"

But the corners of the room were quiet and vacant. Hooker was gone. The door swung to and fro.

Chapter Fourteen

Hooker rode downtown on his bicycle.

Outside the store, he propped the bike against the glass and felt in his pocket for the money. Fifty cents. Afterward he could afford a soda in the Tamblyn's across the road.

He looked inside the store.

Through the windows, Hooker could see that their neighbor, Mrs. Gaylor, was standing talking with another lady he did not know. He looked up at the sign over the door and sighed.

JARMAN'S GROCETERIA—FRUIT AND
VEGETABLES, SUNDRIES SINCE 1927

He went in.

"Hello," he said to Mrs. Jarman, "I've come for paper napkins."

"Oh," said Mrs. Jarman, smiling down from the middle steps of a ladder, "I'll be busy just a minute, Hooker. Isn't Harry there?"

"Yes…he's—"

"Then ask him, will you, dear?"

"Yes'm."

Hooker turned, already fishing for the money in his pocket. He did not like this sort of situation—having to deal with Harry. It made him feel guilty. He did not like other people working unless they were grown people, whose business it was to work.

"I've come for some of those," he said, and pointed broadly at a shelf which contained, as well as the desired napkins, a vast and overt display of toilet paper. He thought of Iris and the telephone—and how simple it would have been for her to do this.

Harry was standing close by with a long and important-looking broom. He wore his own apron which had been given to him, specially made, by his mother. It read "Harry Jarman" in thread across the chest, over the heart.

"Bum wad?" said Harry, with a horrible and knowing smile. Mrs. Jarman was safely and deafly distant.

"No," said Hooker, and then made the mistake of adding, "We have that."

There was more leering as Harry leaned on his broom. Hooker wanted to run.

"Here!" said Harry, and threw, all of a sudden, a roll of the offensive paper at Hooker. "Soft," he added glibly. "Read the label!"

Hooker attempted to be aloof. He held out the roll and slipped it onto the broom stick. Immediately, Harry Jarman unraveled some and pretended to be reading. He bugged his eyes at some terrible inscription, unrolling the paper rapidly as he "read."

"The Midsummer Ball takes place tomorrow, and all the Winslows will be present—'cept of course the

173

nutty ones they don't let out of their rooms...."
Hooker blanched. "Even the youngest Winslow will be
there—and Gil Winslow will, of course, get drunk and
float out through the door...."

Hooker now reddened and choked.

"Janice Parker will be there with both boobs hanging out—"

"She will not! She's gone to Jamaica...." said
Hooker, and then stopped. Harry laughed.

Hooker grabbed the toilet paper violently with both
hands and yanked it away from Harry. The broom
tipped up, and the roll went flying. Suddenly the aisle
was filled with tinted paper.

"What's happened?" said Mrs. Jarman, looking over
from the ladder. "Did something fall?" All she could
see was their heads and shoulders, because they were
two aisles away from her.

"Nothin', Mama. Just some tissue paper spilled."

"Aanh."

She went back to her work.

"Pick it up," said Harry quietly to Hooker.

"I won't!" said Hooker out loud. "I came for napkins. And that's all!"

"Then get them!" said Harry. He had the added
insult, to Hooker's ears, of a changing voice. He knew
that Hooker, being small, could not reach the shelf. He
grinned. His breath smelled of illicit cigarettes. There
was something menacing and nearly adult about him.

"I can't," said Hooker. "You know I can't."

"Well, I'm busy," said Harry. "Why don't you get
your famous big brother to come and reach for them?
Or would he fall down?"

Hooker, without thinking, struck.

Harry yelled.

Mr. Jarman came into the front of the store, and Harry said, "Those damn Winslows are all crazy! They're crazy people!"

He felt his nose. It was bleeding.

Without a word, Mr. Jarman sent Harry to the back of the store.

Hooker was shaking. He felt Mr. Jarman's hand rest lightly on his shoulder.

"How is your mother, Hooker?" he asked with a slight German accent.

Hooker could not answer. All he could think to say was, "She's crazy."

"Did I hear it was napkins you wanted?"

Hooker tried to nod.

"I give you these," said Mr. Jarman. He placed two cellophane packages, which made loud and obvious noises, into Hooker's trembling hands. "Go, then," he said, "I put these on the bill."

Hooker went away, but before he went, he heard something else—Mrs. Gaylor's voice.

"They *are* crazy, you know, all of them. I heard them last night, yelling at each other...."

Hooker ran past her.

As he passed through the door, he could hear behind him the rising voices of Mr. Jarman and Harry, in a mixture of German and English: "Stupid! *Mein Gott, du bist ein*—idiot, Harry!"

The glass door shivered to a closed position, and Hooker heard instead the relatively quiet noises of the street.

Like one, if he were older, who stood in need of a quick drink, Hooker headed, walking blindly, for the Tamblyn's drugstore and a malted.

On the way across the street, he began to clear his mind of the confusing memory of Harry's laughter and concentrated on the hurt of his words.

"Why," thought Hooker furiously, "must everyone know? How do they know? And why should it be funny and make them mean?" His mother had never done anything to anyone—except yell at Mrs. Gaylor once. And Gil had never hurt anyone. He hadn't meant to get into trouble. Or had he? Was there something— were there many things—incidents...occasions...happenings—that Hooker was not aware of? Was this why Gil stayed in the library at home all day? Was he really afraid they would kill him? When was the last time he had gone out in the daytime? Why were they called "crazy people"? And why did Mrs. Gaylor say it, too? Was it what everyone thought?

He reached the marble counter, sat down, and ordered.

"H'lo, Hooker," said a woman he could not remember.

He tried to smile.

"Hear you're going to the Ball this year."

"Yes," said Hooker modestly. "Yes...I am."

"Get you," said the anonymous woman. "Well, it's the do of the season. You ought to have a good time. Got a girl friend, yet?"

"No...no," said Hooker.

"Going to have dancing. And a band."

"Well..."

"Have a good time," said the lady, heading for the door. "You're only young once!"

"I'm nearly twelve...." said Hooker feebly. But the woman was gone, and the screen was slapping back and forth to mark her exit. He had no idea at all who she had been.

He sat there and brooded. Once it had been good to know one or two people and to have them know you, but now it was not good. It was sinister and odd. He did not like the way everyone seemed to know who he was and whom he belonged to and what his family was doing all the time.

His milk shake came. The young girl behind the counter put it in front of him and walked away, tired, to find her check pad. Momentarily she returned and thrust a green slip of paper under his glass. She had written "30¢" on it. It should have been twenty cents. He said nothing. He wanted to cry. He tried to catch the girl's eye, but she paid no attention. By now she was reading a magazine at the other end of the counter.

Hooker finished quickly and walked to the cashier. He held up the bill.

"I had a milk shake," he said.

The woman said, "Okay," and put out her hand.

Hooker, having expected her to notice the error, was confused by her bland acceptance of it and immediately paid the money without question. Except in his eyes.

On his way out, one final thing happened.

He had paused, balancing the napkins, to put the change in his pocket. He was beside the magazine rack. There was a man there who held a magazine.

Hooker stood quite still and silent, and looked up at the man, prepared to smile. But, oddly, the man did not look at him in return, as somehow Hooker had expected he would. And then the crazy, final happening occured.

Swiftly, as Hooker turned to go, he was touched, exactly as though he had been naked, in the soft part of the groin. Fingers, from somewhere, groped immediately and completely—and were gone.

Hooker gasped but was impelled to press himself out through the doors, unaware that he was running, and before he could even remember where he was going, or why, he was there, across the street, panting and out of breath, back beside Jarman's Groceteria.

Slowly, with his back to the drugstore opposite, he dumped the cellophane packs into his carrier and attempted to mount the bicycle.

He became confused. He could not manage it.

What had happened? What was happening? What was happening? What was happening?

What was happening?

What was happening?

What was going to happen…?

Chapter Fifteen

"**Y**ou still figure on coming with me tonight?" Iris said to Hooker at supper.

"Thank you," said Hooker.

"Does that mean yes or no?"

"Yes."

Iris gave a long, worried look at Hooker and then turned to Rosetta.

"Shall I keep a supper warm for Mr. Gil or not?"

"No."

"He ain't been outa there all day," said Iris.

"I'm well aware of that, Iris."

"You know this is my night out?"

"Yes."

Iris paused diplomatically. "Will it be all right?" she finally had to ask.

"I don't see why not," said Rosetta.

Iris looked at Nicholas.

"Go ahead," he said. "We can always call the police if he breaks loose again."

Iris did not appreciate the tone of voice.

"I was only trying to help," she muttered.

Nicholas regarded his plate.

Rosetta said, "Mr. Winslow's sorry, Iris. He didn't

mean to hurt your feelings."

Iris made her way to the swinging door.

"Nine o'clock," she said to Hooker, and disappeared.

"Where are you going tonight?" Rosetta asked.

"Alberta Perkins'," said Hooker. He had a headache.

Rosetta thought for a moment.

"You mean to the Harrises', Hooker?"

"No," said Hooker, looking directly and rudely at Rosetta. "I mean to Alberta Perkins'."

He got up from the table. He felt so odd. He left the room without asking to be excused.

Rosetta waited...but Nicholas did not speak.

She sighed. Could it really be that their father had been dead for thirty-five years? It seemed so unlikely. She started to count.

Surprisingly Gilbert was not asleep.

"What's happened?" he said, as Hooker entered the library. "Did I kill your cat?"

Hooker did not answer. He thought about his headache.

He started fiddling his finger along the bookshelves.

Outside, the evening was almost, but not quite, over.

"Did I kill your cat?" said Gilbert.

The library was still hung with the opaque air of cigarettes and liquory smells.

Hooker felt afraid to answer. He looked at Gilbert.

"Was it the pretty one? The pregnant one?"

"She was red," said Hooker. "You killed her yesterday with your car."

Gilbert in his turn looked at Hooker.

"What was her name, Hookie?"

"Clementine. I feel funny."

"I was terribly pissed," said Gilbert, ignoring what Hooker had said. "Christ, I was pissed! I thought she was a skunk!"

Hooker leaned against the books. The ugly language confused and worried him. It seemed as though everyone used it now. Even his mother had sworn last night.

"Don't lean against the books," said Gil. "You'll break all the covers."

"How can I break all the covers when I'm just in one place?" Hooker said, surprising himself with the volume at which he spoke.

Gilbert fooled around for a match.

"Nobody seems to understand this is really my library anyway," he said. "It's my collection, my books. So, watch out."

He reached under the pillow for a bottle.

"You never let anyone in," said Hooker.

"You get in," said Gil.

"It's smelly," said Hooker. "Who'd want in?"

"Open the window, then."

Gilbert poured a small taste of whiskey. It was rye. He held up the bottle.

Hooker did not open the window. He did not want to move.

"It hasn't the intellectual connotations of wine," said Gilbert of the bottle.

He put it away in another place, under the sofa.

He looked at Hooker.

"Read me the titles," he said.

"I've got a headache," said Hooker.

"If you read them, it will go away."

Hooker turned. There were orange and green and red and blue covers. Some of the writing was in silver and gold, but most in black. When Hooker was learning to read, Gilbert had taught him by getting him to do this.

"Where from?"

"Where you are. Anywhere. Just start there."

Gil lighted another cigarette from the one before and prepared to listen. He put his head down and seemed to smell into his glass.

"I can't see," said Hooker.

"Go on," said Gilbert. "Go on."

Hooker began, "*Lee's Lieutenants*," he said.

"*Leftenants*—*Leftenants*. Jesus, you're not American *yet*."

"*Lee's Leftenants...*" He paused, waiting, and then continued quickly: "*T.E. Lawrence by His Friends... Other Men's Flowers... Hercules My Shipmate... Arundel...Vile Bodies... Scoop...*" Then several titles all in a row, with the appendage, "P.G. Wodehouse." "And *The Wind in the Willows...*"

"Pooh spring cleaning..." Gil muttered. "Bah! Spring cleaning...Pooh!"

Hooker then read a whole shelf of poet's names: "Byron... Shelley... Blake... Scott... Brooke... Arnold... Keats... *The Sonnets of Shakespeare...*" and more. And more...and more...and more.

"*Chums*," he said, by this time out of breath. "*Chums '38...Chums '39...Chums '40...Chums '41... Airplanes of the Future...Jane's...Closets*—"

"Clausewitz!"

182

"—on War...*The Woman of Andros*..."

Gilbert made a drinking noise and reached for more paper. He began to write.

"Go up a shelf and over, left."

Hooker moved, on the command, to the appointed place. He began to feel less peculiar.

"*Tender Is the Night*," he said.

"'Already with thee tender is the night....'" said Gilbert, writing. Cigarette ash dribbled into his glass; he got out the bottle, fitted it lip to lip with the glass, and said, "But it has no intel—*lec*—tual connotations...." Then he wrote this down and smiled. Afterward, he crossed it out and did not smile.

"Go on," he said.

"*The Crack Up*..."

"Yes, yes, yes. Go on." Gil seemed testy, but Hooker did not stop. He continued:

"*The Great Gatsby...Tales of the Jazz Age.... The Far Side of Paradise... The Disenchanted...This Side of Paradise*..."

Gilbert laughed.

Hooker stopped.

"'All right,'" said Gilbert, using a funny, unrecognizable voice, "'so, you're disenchanted... I'm disenchanted ...we are all disenchanted!'" Then he laughed again.

He looked at Hook, but Hooker could not maintain the looking back, and so he went on reading.

"Thurber..." Gilbert muttered. "Very funny man. Dead."

"*The Northwest Passage... The Red Wine of Youth... Anthony*..."

Hooker stopped reading. He looked at Gil.

"Who's dead?"

Gilbert blinked, and then, understanding, he smiled.

"The best of us is dead," he said. "The best of us."

He wrote it down: "The best of us is dead."

He crossed this out and wrote, instead: "The best of us *are* dead."

Watching his brother write, Hooker said, "Gilbert?"

"Yes?"

"What did you do to Janice Parker?"

"Nothing."

"Everyone says you did do something. Even Harry Jarman says you did."

"Then he's a liar."

"But what did you do?"

"I thought you had a headache," Gil said.

"It's gone," said Hooker. "Tell me."

Gilbert sighed and put his hand across his eyes.

"You wouldn't know, even if I did tell you. Not in three-foot letters, you wouldn't know."

Hooker looked out the window.

"Something happened to me today," he said.

"Bravo!" said Gilbert.

"It did, though. I'll tell you if you'll tell me."

"I haven't anything to tell."

Suddenly Hooker burst into tears. He could not hold them back anymore.

"What's the matter?" said Gilbert suspiciously. His mother had cried so often.

"Nobody will tell me anything," said Hooker.

Gilbert tried to laugh.

"Is that all?"

Hooker pouted. He ran his finger along the nearest shelf. There were things, finally, to know. There was something important to tell, at last. But neither would happen now. He stopped crying.

"We might just as well," he thought, "not be people at all." He was thinking of the way they had once been together, of the other families he had known—it seemed so long ago, now. And all those families, and they themselves, had been people.

"Will anyone remember?" he asked.

"Remember what?"

"Mother."

Gilbert took a deep breath.

"Of course they will," he said.

"Will they talk about her?"

"No."

"Will they be sorry about her?"

"Why should they be sorry?"

"Because."

"I think so, then. Yes. *I'm* sorry."

"Will *they* be sorry? Father. Rosetta. Those ones?"

"We'll never know about that."

"Why?"

"Because she will get old, and we will forget. It won't be important anymore."

Hooker put his hands in his pockets.

"I don't want to get old," he said.

Gilbert had to smile.

"Tough," he said. But it did not seem mean for him to say so. Hooker looked at him.

"Couldn't we go out?" said Hooker.

"Where?"

"Into the outside. I want to talk to you."

Gilbert paused.

"I guess we could," he said. "We can go out by the stable."

"Good," said Hooker. "Good."

They carefully collected together what Gilbert wanted to take. They put it all in an overnight bag, as though they were going out for a long time. They put in the remainder of the whiskey in its bottle and a pad of paper. They also put in pencils, a sweater, and some cigarettes.

They went out onto the grass.

"It was a beautiful day. This is a beautiful evening, Hookie," said Gilbert, and paused with his hanky out and slowly wiped his face. Hooker saw the normally hidden recession of the hairline; little beads of water stood in a conical row, down over Gilbert's brow. His white shirt was wet. He looked old.

Gilbert said, "Its so damned hot. It's just incredibly humid. Where are we going?"

The motion of walking seemed to make him tired.

"Hook?"

"Do you want me to carry the bag?"

"No," said Gilbert, "I will—*aaaaagh!*"

He fell. He had tripped by catching his foot in a croquet hoop that had been left in the lawn from all the games they had never played.

"Where are we going?" he said from the ground.

"We ought to go to the stable. Otherwise father might see you. Or Rosetta."

"What?" said Gil, "and *know* I've been drinking!"

Even Hooker had to laugh.

Gilbert, sitting where he was, opened the bag and said, "Let's have a game of croquet. You might as well take advantage of the fact that you've finally caught me out of doors."

"No," said Hooker, "not now. We'll play some other time."

They both laughed again—not knowing why.

Chapter Sixteen

When Hooker had told Gilbert what had happened to him in the Tamblyn's, Gilbert gave a long sigh and then said, "Well."

"So what did it mean?" said Hooker.

But Gilbert did not answer. Instead, he said, "I *am* good for one thing, Hook. Talking. I can talk. Is that agreed?"

"Yes," said Hooker. "That's agreed."

"So I will try to say something. All right?"

Hooker nodded. Perhaps tonight he would tell Gil about the gun, after all.

"If I could only think where I should begin."

Gilbert drank from the bottle.

"Hey, Hook!" he said, laughing, "look't this."

He raised the bottle at the house.

"A toast," he said, "to the NUT HOUSE!"

Then he drank again. He got the giggles again. He lowered his voice.

"Rosetta would pee in her pants if she could see this."

They both giggled, and the giggling was very quiet, almost sinister. Gilbert's eyebrows worked up and down.

"Now be quiet," he said. "Be quiet. This is a serious conversation."

Hooker became quiet, and in a moment, Gilbert stopped giggling, too.

He drank, and the drink ran down his chin.

"Oh, dear," he said. "Oh, dear. Now——let me see...."

He placed a finger on his chin, and posing like that, he looked at the sky and said:

> "When God at first made man,
> Having a glass of blessings standing by—
> 'Let us' (said He) 'Pour on him all we can...."

and then he started to giggle again. Now, the giggle became a laugh.

Hooker became worried. He was afraid that Rosetta or their father would look out and see them.

"Don't," he said. "You'll get caught."

"Caught? In this house!" said Gilbert. "Ridiculous!"

At last, he was serious.

"I must be good for something...." he said.

Hooker waited.

"Don't let it throw you," Gil said. "What happened this morning in the drugstore, I mean. It's all part of getting terribly old." He stared at his feet, smiling.

"It was just so sudden," said Hooker.

"Kinda took you by surprise, eh? Well. Like I say, don't you worry. And the next time it happens, just kick the guy in the balls and run. That'll stop 'im. You see, it's like any impulse—any old impulse. He had an impulse to touch you, and you didn't stop him. Now. That's all right. But you see...some of us..." He paused and then yelled out at the house: "...WANT TO BE STOPPED!" His voice came back to the vicinity of Hooker. "Not from the ordinary things but from the other things—the weak things, like that man touching you or like me not having a job and drinking. I want to be stopped. I want to be. Except—"

He lighted a cigarette.

"It's too late, of course—because, eventually, it is always too late."

"Can't you stop yourself?"

Gilbert looked at Hooker as though amazed, but then, he smiled.

"How?" he said. "In the name of Jesus."

"I don't know, but—"

"No. No. No, no, no... No. After a while there's only one way to stop yourself. Only that one way."

Gilbert raised a hand, and on the hand one finger.

"What way?"

"Unh? Oh. Well. I mean—there is a way to stop, if you want to..."

"I know, but..."

Suddenly, as if he were changing the subject completely, Gilbert said, "I'm not a liar, Hook. You know that. Don't you?"

Hooker listened but did not speak.

"Have I ever told you the story of Mr. Brown at Markham?"

"I don't know. I don't think so."

"Oh, you'll adore Mr. Brown. You will just adore him. How's your headache?"

"All right. Who is he? Mr. Brown."

Gilbert considered this and then said, "God. If you

have never met God, Hooker, you will meet him at Markham College. And his name is Mr. Brown."

Gilbert looked at the ash on his cigarette.

"You see, when I was in school at Markham and I did such things as write poetry, there were a lot of others—Haney and Gould and Richards, all those guys—who studied their books and got to know the answers just by looking at them, and they knew all about how to really succeed in this life. Stupid guys, who had no minds, you realize, but who had the foresight, somehow, to see that all they had to do was memorize the factual part of knowledge and go on from there. You could never call them liars. They never questioned what it was they knew—they simply knew it. There it was in the book. The truth. Now. I could have done that, too, but I didn't. I had to work very hard to get my memory to know anything. Oh, not in my mind—my mind knew things and does still, but not my memory. Always I had to question things: 'Does an isosceles triangle make any sense?,' I'd say. When the book said, 'Here are four positive propositions—one, two, three, and four—and each is correct in its supposition,' I had to go and doubt it. Do you think you see? Well, people in school aren't usually like that, and most of them at dear old Markham look at dear old Mr. Brown, their teacher, and they follow his finger along the board, and they gladly repeat, 'I see the honeybee is making honey while he's mating flowers' or 'Four-and-four makes eight.' And 'Eight-and-eight makes sweet sixteen.' Well"—he shrugged—"they came to knowledge. But I had to count it over in my mind. 'Look, Winslow,' Mr. Brown would say, 'you're slow, you know that? You don't belong in this class here, because you don't even understand that two-and-two make bloody-well four.' He wanted blind obedience to fact, but to me all that meant was the guy had no imagination. I had to wonder. I had wonderment, which means I had all those little, tiny worries that whole days and days of wasted time are made of. I had those, you see—and so, of course, we came to graduation, and I failed. Yes. Two whole years I struggled after all those Brown-nosed facts, and I never did get them straight. *His* way. Then, just before the third time round was over, there was this class in English when I wrote the ballad."

Gilbert paused, remembering. Then slowly he began again.

"Everybody had to write a ballad, you see, and most of the guys wrote very bad poetry—most of their poems were nothing more than rhymed words. But I had one that really—even if *I* say it—had the beat. The Ballad-Beat! Hah! You see? Well, I thought, 'This once I'm proud; this once I'll get to shine. Mr. Brown is going to eat his cake'—you see. And we got to the time of the reading, and I read it—all emotional at last, 'cause there I was, and I knew how good it was, how right it was and how original and excellent it was, and he said, 'I think that's marv'lous, Winslow.'" Gil repeated, "Marv'lous! Marv'lous!"

Hooker smiled and waited.

Gilbert said, "And then he said, 'Where'd you steal it?'"

Hooker made a face.

"That's what he said, though," said Gilbert "See?

You see? He had to break my pride. Every little saved-up Jesus bit."

They sat still.

"Then, of course, I really couldn't stand it, because in one place, just once—in verse—I knew I had a talent. I knew I had a leaning that was true. I'd worked and slaved and sweated on that ballad. And then, 'long comes Brown, and boom, he said I stole it."

Gil looked at Hooker.

"It just wasn't true. It wasn't true. Because I wrote it myself. I really did. So, I called him down. I said, 'I didn't steal that ballad, Mr. Brown, I wrote it.' All the guys believed me, 'cause they knew that I had that kind of mind. But, 'Oh, no you didn't, Winslow, I can even tell you where you stole it from,' he said, and I was shocked. This really shocked me. I thought, 'My God, perhaps in some mad way this could be true. In some weird, long-forgotten way, I might have just remembered what I'd thought I'd made up in my mind.' But the *truth* was that I wrote it. Remember that. So after class the guys all said, 'Oh, sure, old Gilbert Hugo Winslow, it was you wrote it.' And I went down to Garret, the Head, to say that I'd run away if Brown persisted in this lousy lie of that plagiarism. Well, Garret said. '*Now*, Winslow'—he talked like that—'*Now*, Winslow, I'm afraid your record really *shows* that you're not our kind of *student*. I don't know the English poem so well that I'd be *able* to *say* you stole it, but it stands to *reason* that with your *lazy*, uncooperative, fooling *attitude*, Mr. Brown is undoubtedly absolutely *right* about what he claims is *true*, and I'm afraid I'll have to tell your *parents*, Gilbert.'"

Gil paused.

"Well, that's not quite the end of it. Next day, Mr. Brown, in class, said, 'Winslow, I believe you have an apology and a confession to make—will you please stand and do so,' and I said, 'What, sir? No, sir, *I* have nothing to say.' 'Of course you have,' he said, 'about that ballad, and I want you to renege on it here and now—you must admit your guilt before this class, in my presence, I will not accept anything less.' Now the guys thought I must be nuts. 'Why not?' they said. 'We know you wrote it. Tell Brown you're sorry, and he'll forget it.' 'Well, not on your life,' I said. 'I'm sorry, Mr. Brown, sir, Mr. Brown—but you're a bastard' and I just took off and left the class."

Gil thought briefly, and then concluded.

"I got my cigarettes out of my locker, I put on my best blue suit, and I went to town, and I've been here ever since. See? Do you see? That's when I came home, which you probably remember. But now you know, also, why. It's why I think I came home. And that is the important thing, you see. Everyone must think out their stories very clearly."

Later.

Hooker looked at the croquet hoops and the colored stakes.

"What is it I'll need to know," he said, "that everyone keeps talking about?"

Gil looked a little sideways—red-eyed—at him.

"Much there is that surpasses understanding, kid," he said.

"But tell me a little. Even a little."

"I can't tell you a little. There is no 'little' to tell. Know-ing is guessing, I guess. You take a little of what you know, and you pretend you know all the rest of it. You make it up. You have to. Ergo: I cannot tell you anything."

"Why?"

"'Cause all knowledge is that way. It's part the premise and part the experience. And experience is what you make up by yourself."

"Doesn't anybody know anything for sure, then?"

"Yes. They know the facts—as they're called."

"Facts?"

"I mean human thought and human endurance has solidified into what they call facts. And these facts help us to the educated practices, but they don't help us to forget what we are, which is what you're asking about. Like about that man. And me. And Mom and Dad."

"Unh-hunh."

"Factually, we're civilized. See? Factually, you and I are aristocrats."

The stable had dribbled scratchy red paint, old and flaky, onto the ground. Hooker moved some with his finger against the brown of the earth. He rephrased his question:

"Isn't hurting people wrong, then?"

Gil swigged out of the bottle suddenly and then let it down between his knees softly. He shivered.

"Not so long as it's done factually!" Gil laughed. "No," he said, "no—but, really, that is the most loaded...lousy...question of all time, because the answer is presupposed to be yes."

"What do you mean, presupposed to be?"

"Just that. But the facts are, it can't be wrong, 'cause s'many folks indulge in it!"

"Indulge in it?"

"Indulge. It means 'to continue.'"

Hooker thought about it.

Gilbert said, "I think you are really asking me to tell you about sex. But I haven't any good way of telling you about that. Sex is something—one of those things—you make up a story about. It's your life, so you make up your own story. There is no answer—that is, no good explanation. You wonder what all the hurt is for, all that pain they talk about. But there is no hurt. Only shame. We are ashamed not to know, like you, and ashamed when we do know, like me. Men and women, you see— there are men and there are women..."

Hooker waited. Finally he said, "Yes?"

"There are men, and there are women...and..."

Gilbert looked at Hooker. It was odd. It was a frightened look. It was a look of horror, but Hooker could not understand it. Gilbert was crying.

"What's the matter? What's wrong? What is it?"

Gilbert said, "I don't want you to know. Oh, Jesus— I don't want you to have to know things!"

Hooker looked away.

Then Gilbert said, "Hook?"

"Yes?"

"When I told you I am not a liar, did you believe that?"

Hooker swallowed.

"Yes," he said.

"And did you believe me about the poem?"

"Yes."

"And would you believe me if I said it wasn't me—not me and Janice Parker?"

"Yes."

Gilbert watched the back of the house.

"And..."

"Yes?"

Pause.

"Hook?"

"Yes?"

"Hook?"

"Yes?"

"Do you ever get a feeling of—do you ever feel as though something funny was going to happen to you, Hook? Like something you are afraid of?"

Now they did look at each other, but Hooker did not speak. Gilbert tried to smile when he saw Hooker's eyes, but he did not make the smile really happen.

So he said very gently instead, "Yes," he said, "so do I," he said. "So do I. So do I. Do you see?"

"Are we crazy people?" said Hooker.

It was sudden.

But Gilbert did not laugh. He softened his voice right down.

"How do you mean that?" he asked.

"Seriously," said Hooker. "I want to know."

Gilbert sighed. The stable was like a soft red wall behind them, and over the lawn anyone could come and gently stumble over the hoops that were placed there for a game. But no one did come—just a few birds, and they were worming, and they were careful, for to them the hoops were nothing more than mantraps that they must be shy of. The sun glimmered faraway and yellow. It became moist, and the air was heavy with the scent of grass, marigold leaves, and old wicker chairs. Hooker could also smell the smoke of Gilbert's cigarette, which was the smell of gray wood very lightly on fire, he thought, and something mysterious.

Hooker said, "Mother is upstairs and won't come down. You live in the library. Rosetta won't look at me. Iris has secrets. And Papa sits with his back to everything. What does it mean?"

"Oh," said Gilbert, "I don't know."

"Mrs. Gaylor says we're crazy."

There.

Gil put down the bottle. He looked off over the hoops.

"The object of the game," he thought, "is to get through all the way and beat your opponent to the stake."

Out loud he said, "Mrs. Gaylor, eh?"

"Yes," said Hooker.

There came a deep silence. Hooker found it made him sorry he'd spoken—afraid.

Gilbert touched the bottle gently. He swung it in at his crotch and looked at its tip. He stuck his finger in and lifted the bottle up off the ground.

"You'll break it," said Hooker, "and cut off your finger."

Gilbert let the bottle down.

"Hooker," he said, "tell me. What is crazy?"

Hooker paused.

"Nutty, I guess. Like funny. Not doing things right. I don't know. All I know is—*crazy*."

He looked at Gil sharply.

"Just crazy," he repeated.

And Gilbert sighed and looked away.

"What is it you want?" he asked. "Something sane?"

"I don't know," said Hooker. "I'm not asking."

"Yes, you are!"

"Don't get mad. I only meant—"

"You're a stinking little queer. Why didn't you hit Old Lady Gaylor in the mouth?"

"But what does it mean?" said Hooker. He did not bother to explain that he had hit Harry Jarman.

Gilbert said nothing. He brooded violently, but his anger toward Hooker, personally, seemed to subside.

"People all know you don't *do* anything."

Gilbert removed his finger from the bottle and drank very quietly. Hooker took a chance and goaded for an answer.

"And Harry Jarman says we're crazy, too."

"Talk on," said Gilbert, looking odd all at once, with his legs stretched out that way, and his shoes so neatly polished.

"So, I think that we are crazy people," said Hooker. "Like those crazies in the asylum. We have a crazy mother, don't we?"

"Oh, Jesus," said Gilbert.

"It's like a whole list of crazy people, and we're the last of them—don't you think?"

Gil had a mouthful of answers but could not speak. He sat still.

Hooker looked at him. He knew that it was all true, what had been said. About the poem at school. About the cat. About their mother. About Janice Parker. What Mrs. Gaylor had said. He saw Gil's shoes and his gray, neat trousers, pressed, and he saw his hands, without hair, and he saw the funny but aristocratic nose and the open, wordless mouth. He saw the chinless vastness of his brother's neck and his blue, blue, washed-out eyes and the bottle and the receding hairline. He heard a few, quick, softened words from the past—words Gil had said: "Good night—you can call me if you want me." They whispered over the lawn, under the treacherous hoops, bowled like a ball that missed the stake, and he knew at last that it was true. They were crazy people, just as it had been said, and he himself, sitting there, up against the old red stable with a crazy brother, and the sound of the buzzing wings in his ears—he was the last.

So, the evening saddened into silence.

"It's late so early now," said Gilbert. "And so cool. You should go in. Go on with Iris. I'll sit here, just a little. I like this view. I've always liked this view across the lawn. I like the view of our old house. And the trees and everything."

"I'm sorry," said Hooker. "I didn't mean it personally."

Gilbert smiled.

"I know," he said. "It's just your funny way of talking. That's all, kid. You talk funny. But at least you talk. Good night."

"Good night."

It became completely dark.

Chapter Seventeen

On the way to the country club, Hooker rode in the back seat. His father drove.

The road was practically empty all the way, which was surprising for a Friday, and after they had left the highway and turned onto the old, country part of the way, there was not a sign of traffic.

Nicholas drove swiftly. He leaned into the door and hung one elbow out the window. He felt easy, and his wrists, as he drove, were loose. He smoked. The collar of his shirt was open.

Rosetta, sitting in the passenger seat up front, was apparently completely engrossed in thought. Her forehead was skinned down toward her eyes, and her eyebrows were looped like little dumped parentheses. Her mouth was pursed. She gloved and ungloved her hands as though she were trying to see how many times she could do it before they arrived. It made Hooker apprehensive.

Beside him, on the back seat, were two suitcases and an overnight bag. In the bag were Hooker's own blue suit, a shirt, knee socks, and a pair of black oxford shoes. In one suitcase, Nick's dinner jacket and trousers, shoes, shirt, and accessories lay, and in the other—a much larger, flatter suitcase—could be found Rosetta's blue-velvet gown, slippered dancing shoes, and a jeweled evening bag with a long gold chain. Inside the handbag, Hooker knew, would be a pearl cardcase, a sachet envelope, and two handkerchiefs of lace.

They drove on. The embattled trees were losing ground to the summer's drought. The sky was still as white and hot as it had been all season, and the lack of rain gave a dry and dusty smell to the woods, as they passed.

Stones threw themselves up at the underside of the car as it raced along. Hooker could feel his old fear of speed returning in his stomach.

But they soon would be there.

They passed by row on row of crooked, snake-rail fences and a few patches of forest. There were birch trees, maples, oaks, diseased elms, and beech. There came and went an apple orchard with an overpowering deep-sweet aroma—an orchard that crouched in jagged lines behind a wall and made Rosetta gasp, perhaps at some old remembrance.

There was a meadow so thick with daisies that it seemed like a crop that some farmer had put there to harvest. And there were bees—the golden, fat kind that seem to be asleep but which are habitually busy, working as though in a trance, hypnotized by their labor.

There was one milk-green butterfly sitting in the yellowy dust of the road. Nicholas swerved the car to avoid it, and they all watched it as it floated away unaware, almost without beating its wings.

The road looped…fell…and began its final rise before the turn through the woods that would signal their arrival.

Rosetta left one glove on and one in her gray-wool lap. They were white. With her ungloved hand she adjusted her hair net—a coarse one, not the color of her hair.

She said, "They've taken down some of these trees. Do you see?"

But no one replied.

The woods were being thinned of condemned elms, which were diseased.

The gates appeared. These were pillars of stone, and the irons were huge. They stood open.

TEN MILES PER HOUR. THANK YOU, said an immodest sign. The THANK YOU had been considered a mark of good taste.

Hooker slid low until he was almost flat out. He looked out the window and up at the motion of the sky beyond the branches. Nicholas had slowed to twenty, but they seemed to be going very fast, as Hooker viewed the trees.

Gradually the woods and their enclosure began to dissipate, and Hooker sat up to see the last part of the road, which he always liked. This was just at the final dip, before the hazardous twist which led to the top.

Always the car felt as though it were going to roll sideways when it reached the pit of this indentation. It was necessary to increase speed, and they did so. The car sprouted sudden wings, voomed loudly, and rose— as if jettisoned—courageously around the corner in a dance of balance, and fled up to the crest, where the road and then the view broke into the open and freed itself of the last trees in the wood. And then...a large, Jacobean old brick-and-beam mansion appeared. This was The Club.

Before its walks there was an open parking lot of crunched stone, and around three sides there was an almost formal cloister of Scotch pines and spruce trees. Under these trees could be seen, in sun patches, the tartan-and-leather colors of the members' golf bags, each of which was sitting on its own cart.

Nicholas braked. In the immediate silence which followed, they heard the wind in the pines, and for a moment, they sat quite still, all three of them, plainly glad to have arrived in a favorite place. They saw Gilbert's car at some distance, parked beneath the trees. Hooker looked at it, and it made him feel lonely to see it there—solitary, polished, and red. It looked to him splendid and empty.

They got out. Beneath their feet the gravel swayed and gave way like the sea. All three of them walked about the car, lifting things—all kinds of personal things as well as the suitcases and the bag—out into their arms. Each was loaded down as they approached the building.

Deeply engrossed in her own performance, Rosetta tramped off toward the door which was marked: WOMEN'S LOCKER ROOM AND SHOWERS— PLEASE REGISTER GUESTS. She did not speak.

Nicholas threw away his cigarette and had just offered his hand in the direction of the door when the door was opened by an attendant.

They went through and were immediately cooled

and soothed by the calm insides of the building.

From the end of a long, green, and paneled hallway, which was hung with prints and lettered instructions to the members, they could hear the hiss and the hum of the members' shower room.

Hooker took a deep breath.

A waiter in a white coat passed them, carrying a tray of soft-drink mixers in little, opened bottles. He also had a large jug of ice. He shifted, dancing sideways but without changing pace at all. Hooker admired his feet.

The attendant said, "I'll take those, Master Hooker. H'lo, Mister Winslow. Let me take that to your locker."

He loaded himself gracefully with the major portion of either burden and waited for them to go on beyond him, down the hall.

They started out.

Hooker hated it.

He could hear the laughter as they approached the pinewood lockers in their benched rows. They passed a man in his underwear, who was combing his hair. Little drops of water spun out over Hooker's face as he passed. The shower-room doors were closed. They walked on—Nicholas severe, the attendant busy and thoughtless, Hooker wishing he was in the field with his cats or anywhere beyond these walls.

Nicholas spoke a few greetings. Each seemed inordinately loud to Hooker, as though all his father's friends must be deaf. Abruptly, he was introduced to a man in a droopy towel. Afterwards, he scurried to his father's locker and sat down on the bench.

"Would you like a glass of milk?" said Nicholas.

Hooker said, "Yes."

The attendant smiled, deposited their belongings, and disappeared.

Luckily, there was no one in their row. They did not have to undress completely, anyway, as they only had to unpack a few things and change their shoes.

"When are you meeting your friends?" Hooker asked.

"They're here," said Nicholas. "You can go and meet Rosetta as soon as you're ready."

Already, he was engulfed and drowned in the prospect of what he was to do. Now he was just talking, as he busied himself changing his socks and his shoes, and getting out his golf glove and some old handkerchiefs.

"What are you going to do? Did you see anyone? Probably Rosetta will be having tea later—you can order lots of toast. When you want to, come back and take a shower. Just ask for some towels. But you must be dressed and ready by six o'clock. We don't want to be late."

"No, sir."

"See if you can find Gilbert."

"I saw his car."

"He is here, then?"

"Of course," said Hooker.

"Yes, of course," said Nicholas. "And don't go swimming."

"I didn't bring a suit," said Hooker.

"Oh, well, when Rosetta and her friends nap, you'll find lots of interesting birds out in the woods."

Nick's voice, as usual, was flat and lifeless.

"You're sure you don't want to come round with me?"

Hooker knew he did not mean it.

"Yes, I'm sure."

"Yes. You'd get tired."

"Yes," said Hooker. "Yes, I would."

Nicholas straightened.

"Well," he said.

When he walked away, Hooker did not follow. He remained, still and waiting.

He sat there, with his shoe laces undone, feeling afraid. In a while his glass of milk came. He sat drinking it and thinking.

Then he just sat there—listening carefully.

The first hole on the course was famous throughout Canada. It was even known to many of the American pros, and once it had been written about, with accompanying photograph, in *Sports Illustrated*. It was called the toughest first hole in golf. But it was also famous for the beauty of the vista from the tee. People called it a typically Canadian view. Trees, grass, and distance.

Hooker had found Gilbert near there and had followed him to the empty fairway. Now he watched his brother, who was apparently looking for something in the grass. Perhaps he had lost a ball—except that he did not have his clubs with him.

What was he doing?

Hooker, in the trees, saw Gilbert turn toward the woods, shade his eyes from the sun, and look off and down the hill. He began to pace off the distance between the teeing green and the edge of the hill.

Hooker saw him counting: "One...two...three...four
...five..." right up to twenty-two. Twenty-two yards.
What did it mean?

Gilbert, standing now right on the verge, looked
down, no longer needing to shade his eyes, and he
seemed to be calculating how many trees there were
between where he stood and the road, which ran on
up the valley to the clubhouse, through the woods.

Then Gilbert lighted a cigarette. He stood very still,
smoking, with his eyes half open.

Hooker thought, "He's making up a poem."

Gilbert shifted on his feet like a cripple, not bending his knees—shifting, really, from the pelvis—reset-
ting his heavy torso on its base of spindly, unshaped
legs.

"The poem is about trees," Hooker thought.

Gilbert put his hands in his pockets. His expression
changed. He fully closed his eyes, and the lines on his
face smoothed away, leaving flat, sunlit planes of flesh,
a little wet with perspiration—but no longer per-
turbed, free-looking and even healthy, however pale.

"He likes the poem," Hooker thought. "He's finished it. Maybe later, in the car, he'll write it down in a
book."

Gilbert walked away, then, and Hooker began to
look for a pheasant he had heard calling, earlier, in the
undergrowth.

Soon it would be time to get ready.

Hooker had never before been aware that there was
anything sinister about nakedness. He had never been
intrigued by it. He had seen naked people simply as

people without clothes.

He had seen the boys at school. He had no particular memory of them at all. He and Gilbert had swum together in the lake at St. Cloud with nothing on, and that was not so long ago, and no one had spoken then—nothing had been said, then, or done.

But now it was different, and the difference had something to do with his experience in the drugstore yesterday.

But why must he be afraid, and why was there suddenly something menacing about the mere thought of it?

It was, he thought, only a man's hand. That is what it was. But there was a secret in the look of the man's eyes and a secret in the touch of his fingers. It was because, as a stranger, this man had known something about Hooker that Hooker did not know about himself. About himself. Something dangerous. Something that touched Hooker's mind just as his body had been touched—by something outside itself.

It was like a secret communication from a club. Something in code. A question. Or an answer.

But what? What was he being asked? And what was the response?

For the first time in his life, Hooker began to have an awareness of the difference between each man and the other. He knew, too, that he was different and that his own particular and private inquisitiveness—that was what made him so. His eyes could reveal it. His mind, moving like the man's fingers over things in his imagination—this could betray him. Through what he said and did, and where he looked. And how.

He sat in the locker room, wearing his underwear and taking off his socks.

His father was not there. But he would probably be back shortly. Still, his absence demanded that Hooker move on his own, without the protection or animation of conversation.

Around him, in his own aisle and in the aisles of lockers near at hand, the men were gathering. There was excitement. Their day on the course or in the pool had been gratifying. The weather had been perfect. It was not like a day in any other time of the year. They were also excited by the prospect of the evening before them. Liquor bottles appeared. There was laughter, and there began to be nakedness.

Someone was singing:

> "Roll me *o*-ver
> In the *clo*-ver,
> Do—do—do—
> Do it *again*!
>
> Roll me *o*-ver,
> Roll me *o*-ver..."

Somebody laughed. It sounded like Harry Jarman. Of course, it could not be. But it was that kind of laugh.

They were in the next aisle—the extension of Hooker's own. There were five of them, and they were young—not much older or younger than Gilbert.

Somebody else said, "Have you heard the one about the two happiest guys in the Navy?"

"No. Who?" said a voice.

"Gerald Fitzpatrick—and Patrick Fitzgerald..."

The laughter that greeted the joke grew and grew until it seemed to Hooker like the laughter he had heard in the funny house at the C.N.E. Midway. It was coarse, and it meant something secretly understood, but it was mechanical. And it was dirty. He had heard people laugh like that after telling a sex joke. Even Gilbert.

"Hey. You'd better shut up," said one of the young men. "There's a kid over there."

It was Tony Blair. He smiled. He was the only one of the group that Hooker knew by sight. He was sitting, stark naked, with one leg crooked up on the bench, facing Hooker. Hooker caught himself watching, and he turned away. He heard Tony say, "It's just the little Winslow kid."

"Yeah?"

"I thought he was older than that."

"That's Gilbert."

The voices dropped. Then their laughter rose again. They had made another joke. About Gilbert. Or about his mother.

Hooker stood up.

He had to go to the shower room naked. That was where the towels were. But it was better to go there than to stay here. He was afraid, now, of everyone.

The waiters in their green jackets moved about with trays of ice cubes, glasses, and soda water. They did not seem to see him. He walked slowly, certain that he would run. And he knew that if he ran, they would all know why.

His father appeared. He was with two men, one of his own age and one younger. He stopped Hooker with a gesture.

"Hooker," said Nicholas, "come here."

Hooker approached them.

"I want you to meet two very old friends," said Nicholas. "This is Mr. Morris, Hooker, and this is Mr. Tait." He turned to the men. "My youngest son Hooker," he said with a smile.

The men put out their hands at him. First, Mr. Morris, the older one...

"Hello, Hooker. I'm glad to meet you," he said. "Your father spoke to me about you."

"How-do-you-do?" said Hooker.

Mr. Morris beamed.

Mr. Tait put one hand on Hooker's bare shoulder and shook hands with the other. His fingers, Hooker thought, were warm and dreadfully personal, and he was afraid they were going to slip. They were hairy.

"Hello, little man," he said.

"How-do-you-do?" said Hooker.

There was a silence.

Nicholas wanted to go. He edged away.

"Don't be long, Hooker," he said. "We must all be ready to meet Rosetta on time at six o'clock."

"Yes, sir."

But Mr. Tait said, "A very good-looking little boy, Nick. You should be proud."

They all looked at him.

"Lovely," said Mr. Morris, who could say that sort of thing without sounding affected. "Just like his mother."

"He's got a bad back," said Nicholas after a moment.

"Nonsense," said Mr. Tait. "He looks healthy as a horse."

"Well, he has a bad back," Nick insisted. "See?" He turned Hooker sideways.

"All I can say," said Mr. Tait with a particularly knowing smile, obviously meant to encourage Hooker, "is that the girls had better watch out when *he* grows up." He laughed. He put his hands in his pockets and rose onto his toes.

"Well..." said Nicholas, "except his back. Eh, Hook?" He smiled.

Hooker said nothing. He did not know what his father meant.

"What happened?" said Mr. Morris, as though he, too, saw something that was wrong.

"We don't know. He just grew that way," said Nicholas, patting his son's head. "Like Topsy."

"Well," Mr. Tait was heard to speak last, as they moved away, "I wouldn't put it past him to outstrip us all."

As Hooker turned into the shower room at last, he could hear a fresh burst of laughter. It was the laughter he could recognize—his father, Mr. Tait, Tony Blair.... They were laughing at him. Or at something about him. Wasn't it what Mr. Tait had just said?

It probably was. But again, the meaning—the *meaning*—was not there. Only the words, sounding new. And there was nothing wrong with his back at all.

Hooker did not shower. He went into an adjoining toilet instead. He flushed it and took the clear water, and he put it over his head. Then he cleaned his hands in it, threw some on his shoulders and stomach, dipped his feet in the bowl, and emerged. He took a large, neatly folded towel from a shelf. He did not dry himself but went instead, wet as he was, back to the locker room. He was wrapped from head to foot in the towel.

"You look funny," said his father. "Are you all right?"

"I'm fine," said Hooker. He gave a false and violent shiver. "It's just that I'm cold."

"You won't be when you're dressed," said Nicholas, turning his back. "I think there's going to be chicken à la king for supper. Later on, you can dance with Aunt Rosetta. They'll play a waltz, for certain." He turned back. "You know how to waltz, don't you? That's the simple one. And it's always the most fun."

Chapter Eighteen

Hooker had seen Gilbert walking at the edge of the dancers, picking his way with uncertain steps across and around the wide hems of the ladies' gowns. Like all the other men present, he was dressed entirely in black and white, but it was possible to pick him out at a distance because of his height. He seemed to be in a hurry. And he seemed to be looking for someone.

The music waltzed up noisily behind Hooker, who was standing very near the orchestra.

He watched the dancers as they went. He watched the tiptoed men. He watched the sweep of women's skirts as the whole room sped around him.

All the figures swept along in circles, stepping past. And he watched Gil moving, too.

The two circles—Gilbert's and the dancers'—countered each other.

It was a classical waltz that the orchestra was playing, deep and sweeping, and Hooker, his eyes twisting until they hurt, tried to follow the passage of his brother as he traversed the room. Finally, somewhere, a door flew open, and Gilbert was gone.

Hooker himself began to move. He walked toward

the terrace. It was difficult going, but at last he gained
a place near the big French doors.

Outside was a bar with bartenders in green.

Now, everyone's voice was in tune with the music.
They laughed, and they gabbled, everyone speaking
with incredible speed, but all the words that he heard
were gone before he could decipher them.

Even the breezes that swayed the lamps seemed to
have been caught by the rhythm of the music, and they
swayed and tilted the little rose-and-gold lanterns,
backward and forward, and in and out, half turning,
half bobbing, and all the time there was the sound of
glass pieces touching, in little echoless gestures of
applause, from where the crystals of the candelabra
caught themselves and were entangled in the wind and
would have billowed but were made of glass.

Hooker looked out, and there was Gilbert, trying to
maneuver closer to a man whom Hooker recognized
from his pictures in the paper—Railroad Parker. He
was standing with the Harrises. Instinctively, Hooker
looked to see if he held a shotgun behind his back. But
the oddest thing was the presence, there, of Rosetta—
in spite of Mr. Parker. She stood to one side, her face
locked in a full seizure of angry embarrassment. Too
late to move away, she had seen Gilbert approaching.

Gilbert bowed. His lips moved. Hooker could
guess what he had said. He had flattered Mrs. Harris'
appearance. And to Mr. Parker he also said something
pleasant.

Then Hooker saw the Harrises rivet their gaze on
Mr. Parker, but Rosetta, her little hands reaching in
either direction, one in greeting and the other in

farewell, touched the Harrises and Mr. Parker away, and stepped in alone toward Gilbert.

Hooker saw her say, "Gilbert!" and he saw Gilbert say, "Aunt Rosetta."

Hooker knew of Gilbert's sense of drama when drunk, but he did not guess at his brother's present sense of desperation.

Some had. Like the Harrises, who had moved Mr. Parker into the center of a group of their friends. Mr. Parker seemed confused by their concern.

Hooker was aware of the breeze on his legs. He was standing quietly, right on the verge of either place— the room full of dancers and the terrace filled with watchers.

He tried now to continue to lip-read what his aunt and his brother were saying. But it was impossible. Rosetta was completely frozen and the ice-blue color of her velvet dress seemed to accentuate the chilled expression on her face. Her little handbag glittered on her arm. Gilbert was smiling too much, and the shape of all his words was the same—and wide. But Hooker could see, by their eyes alone, that their argument was beyond mere family bickering now. It was somehow deadly. Shocking and not at all disguised in its meaning. It was no longer safe, for it had leaped over the bounds of pretense, as it had at the dinner table with his father.

Hooker tried to move closer without being seen. It was possible only because of the press of exhausted dancers, newly arriving from the ballroom. They surged outside into the air, laughing and pushing and talking—unaware.

Rosetta was watching Gilbert eagerly, like a snake that is content to wait before it strikes. She seemed, now, to be oblivious of the crowds of people close at hand. She stood, blue and motionless, watching her nephew. Her hands were folded.

"...and if my aim," Gilbert was saying, "had been to 'compromise' his damn daughter, don't you think I could have done it?"

Rosetta did not answer.

"I only came here to prove finally that I *didn't* do it. Isn't that what you want me to prove?"

He smiled.

"You're going to be sorry for this, Gilly," said Rosetta. It was evident that she was repeating herself.

"No," said Gilbert. "No. I won't."

"*We* shall."

"Yes, you will. You'll get down on your hands and knees, and force everyone to regret it, won't you? When in any other light they might just look on it quite simply as it's intended—a defense. Of myself. Like anybody'd make."

There was a long and dangerous pause. People had stopped to listen.

Gilbert's eyes took in the listeners and pulled up, as though braked, upon Rosetta. Then he raised his voice and addressed Mr. Parker, across the distance that separated them.

"Will you openly accuse me? In front of these people?"

Rosetta looked over at Mr. Parker, standing in the circle of her friends, and then turned slowly to face Gilbert.

"Very well," said a voice. "Yes. You are accused. In front of these people."

There was a clap of silence.

Nicholas had appeared and spoken. An odd, shuffling movement spread in waves across the terrace.

The music, having died out, rose now in a sunburst of Viennese gallantry and charm. It seemed to announce that the little scene had come to an end, and the effect it had was to move a large group of laughing people off toward the ballroom, leaving the terrace free but for a few of the principal listeners.

The noises faded as the doors were closed, and all that could be heard now were the sounds of the bartenders, going about their business—the clicking of glasses and bottles close together, and the distant, drifting waltz.

"One of us must move," Gilbert said to Rosetta, taking in his father's presence with a glance.

Mr. Parker turned away, very pale.

A little tapping of nerves made Hooker close his eyes.

When he opened them, Rosetta had taken a step away from Gilbert, toward the Harrises, and as she did so, her arm swung out, and her little jeweled evening bag fell down onto the stones, unnoticed.

Except by Gilbert.

He bent to retrieve it, calling, "Rosetta," holding it softly out toward her—but she was gone into the Harris enclosure, and they and she and Mr. Parker, in a ring of safety and confusion, moved to one of the bars.

Nicholas and Hooker and a few strangers were left. But Gilbert no longer saw them. His fingers clutching the bag, he crossed to Rosetta and forced it upon her, and then, with a nod at Mr. Parker, he turned swiftly and went away in the direction of the parking lot

Rosetta fingered her hair with a languid, almost comic, gesture. She then recovered her poise and stepped toward the bar. Hooker heard her ordering a drink, and in a moment he heard forced laughter rising from beyond a screen of unknown and tuxedoed men.

Nicholas, obviously aware that Rosetta was there, stood still. He did not watch or join her. He lighted a cigarette instead. Hooker wondered why the waltz continued.

He sat down on the stone steps.

"If you go on sitting there on those cold stones, you'll get piles," said Nicholas. "Why the hell don't you go inside?"

"Oh, I'm all right," said Hooker.

They looked at each other, but Nicholas pretended that nothing had happened and went away.

Hooker watched him disappearing across the terrace. His shoulders were hunched forward in a loose, odd way, and his head was poked out to the front, and his hands hung down, each with its own little burden—a glass and a cigarette. He had never seen his father walk that way before. He seemed almost conscientiously ignored by all, and Hooker felt powerless to break the spell of his own silence.

"It's just as if he has no one to talk to," Hooker thought. "Not even me—and I'm sitting right here. And it's because we're crazy."

Rosetta laughed. One of the men near her laughed, as well.

Hooker smelled the air. It was warm and alive with the smell of leaves and cigarette smoke and women's perfume. It felt very close about him and exciting. He felt the old longing to know things and not to wonder anymore. He wondered what all secrets were. In all houses, all families, was it true that no one really loved? Was fear, then, was craziness absolutely everywhere?

"But if I could do what Gilbert did, in front of all these people," thought Hooker, "I wouldn't be afraid anymore."

And then the waltzing stopped.

Somehow the night lighted up with noise and fire.

Chapter Nineteen

A lot of people ran quickly from the building.

From doors and windows, large streamers of golden light cut out into the dark, like knives slicing and slashing at everything black, pushing wedges of illumination onto the grass and the flower beds and the gravel.

Hooker, at first, sat still.

He saw Nicholas turning, very slowly, and saw him wincing at the intrusion of this noise that was everywhere.

Rosetta was dressed in blue forever, reaching delicately along the length of her own arms until she had Mr. Harris by the hand and then just stopping altogether.

At first there was noise....

And then Hooker did not hear anything further.

Everyone had fallen silent and was running quietly. They ran like people in a noiseless dream, in a travesty of altered speed. The women's dresses billowed out in a rustle of taffeta and silk, and the men, in white and black, were silent, crepe, cut-out dolls, blowing in the wind.

The twenty-two yards of fairway that Gilbert had counted off, earlier in the afternoon, were furrowed now with two deep ruts, and some of the people, approaching, fell down on their hands and knees over them, but still no one spoke or cried out or even whispered that they had hurt themselves.

At the edge of the woods—the edge, also, of the hill—there were two scarred trees, lighted with fire where the Jaguar had passed through, and all down the slope, trees and bushes and undergrowth had been pushed aside, as though a bulldozer, berserk, had run away without its driver.

Below, the Jaguar sat on its taillights, propped up against an oak tree, two thirds of the distance to the road.

Gilbert, on fire, lay back like Peter crucified, hooked by his feet to the cross of the motor car, his arms spread out in a hopeless gesture, his head to one side.

In the flames, Hooker saw the shapes of Gilbert and the car for an instant only, before a second explosion, less forceful than the one heard on the terrace, threw the woods and its watchers into confusion and panic.

But immediately there was silence again, except for the quiet inflection of the flames as they stuttered indecisively in the undergrowth and then caught hold and flared.

Far away came the sound of civilized alarm. Someone must have telephoned, because the fire trucks were coming from the town, along the road, past the orchards.

Hooker, covered with dust and brown dirt, slid, dazed, all the way down the path blazed by the car, until he was as near as he could get.

The cross was shattered and vacant.

He found Gilbert—unrecognizable, blackened yet undeniable—in the midst of a patch of ferns and myrtle. His clothing smouldered and was hot to the touch.

Hooker, his mouth open, his face wet with perspiration and fear, lay suddenly beside what he knew was Gilbert, now, and held him by the shoulders with his hands. He stared around him at the people.

And then Nicholas came and pushed Hooker aside—not cruelly, but necessarily—and the lapels of Gilbert's jacket, on fire again, stuck to the palms of Hooker's hands, and he beat them on the ground until they went out.

"Let me cover him," Nicholas said. "Let me cover him....I have a very warm coat—I can cover him up."

Nicholas removed his evening jacket and placed it squarely over Gilbert's ruined face. The arms spread themselves above his head—he looked like a giant insect, pinned to the ground, its six legs sprawled about it in a chaos of futility.

Nicholas rose and started up the hill.

Then he stopped, and said, "How did he get the car onto the fairway? Does anyone understand? How did he do this?"

He blinked at the fellow members of his club and at their wives. And they, in their turn, blinked innocently back. No one spoke.

And then Nicholas went back to the terrace.

The firemen stood about in groups, holding useless lengths of hose, and one of them with an extinguisher

was putting out one of the small fires in the undergrowth. The other people stood and stared.

Hooker looked at the curl of his brother's fingers
and narrowed his eyes at the length of quiet body on
the ground, under its covering. The way he lay was
completely careless, and Hooker wondered how it was
that somehow Gilbert's shoes were never scuffed or
dirty, wherever he happened to walk.

Inside the club, Hooker walked down the green
hall.

His feet went down into thick, deep rug.

"One of us is dead," he thought.

The best of us are dead.

He dwelt, for one enlightened moment, on the pos-
sibility of all knowledge. But it was so small a thought
in itself that he did not stop to consider it.

At the end of the hall, the shower room was empty.

Hooker went in and took off his clothes and turned
on the water.

He stood there, wishing somebody would come.

After Iris had gone away and it was dark in the
room, Little Bones got onto the bed.

Hooker doodled his fingers, very lightly, with a circular motion, down over the base of her spine. He felt
her tail sweep up into a hardened plume. She squeaked
approvingly and afterwards lay in against his legs,
which he had curved to make a nest for her.

"Gilbert is dead," he said to her.

She started to purr.

Hooker's head ached.

Dead people were very faraway, he thought. He thought of them as being at sea—but not in boats, just floating. Every one of them was by himself, and all their eyes were closed, but they could hear, and they could think. The baby...Gilbert...Clementine...the birds...the squirrel...mice...his grandparents...John Harris... And all the time, being dead, they thought about life and wished about it, in a brooding, worried way, because it was never attainable again, and they could never talk to anyone about it or stop being lonely. They just drifted, and sometimes Hooker had dreams about them, which was the only time he saw them.

And yet they were peaceful, because of the peaceful way they lay so still and because of the peaceful way their hands were in repose, quiet and open, with the fingers lightly curled—like Gilbert's. And the only place you could see the pain of their being dead was between their eyes. They all looked so deep in thought—even Gilbert, who had never looked like that in life.

As far as heaven was concerned, it was cold and clear, and in Hooker's brain, the stars there made a noise like the humming of electrical machines, and in the whole sky, everything whirled in circles but drifted without plan.

Suddenly he thought, "Now I have the gun. For Armageddon. It is mine."

Little Bones yapped.

"Sometimes," he thought, feeling her head come up into an alert position, "she is just like a dog."

His fingers moved over her ears, which were stiff

and pointed. She arched the undersides of her cheek-bones into the curve of his palm, rolling her head softly from side to side. He withdrew his hands because they were burned and sore.

"Little Bones is the best of them all," he said to himself.

She had a completely delicate and carelessley thrown together frame, over which her skin and coat hardly seemed to fit. And she was so light that Hooker felt you should be able to see through her if you held her up to the sun. In the daylight, her eyes were the color of caramel milk glass, and the black-brown lines drew them back, like those of an Egyptian cat that he had seen once in a hieroglyph. His other cats had eyes you could see through, but not Little Bones. Her eyes were opaque and queer, and Hooker believed that there was someone old and dead inside her, which made it impossible for her to die.

From downstairs, some voices drifted up to his ears—Aunt Rosetta... Father... Iris...a policeman.

Everything, and everyone, was faraway.

He watched the crack where a shallow beam of light lay under his door. He could smell the leaves outside his open windows. And the house itself smelled of cigar smoke, for one of the policemen detectives, who had accompanied them all home, had smoked a large, fat panatela in a holder.

Little Bones let Hooker scratch her ears and settled back down by his leg.

Policemen were funny. They tried so hard to be nice, and yet they were so terribly stiff and cold and embarrassed that Hooker wanted to laugh at them.

Did it hurt to die?

It made him afraid again. It did hurt—he knew that. It would be like a terrible burn or like a lot of knives jabbing into you. It would be much worse than the pain he felt in his scorched hands.

It would make you feel heavy, and it would make you go deaf.

Hooker wondered—and it was almost an idle thought at first—what it did feel like, and after a moment, he lay his face sideways into the pillow, which he drew gently across and over his nose and mouth. But he could still breathe.

"I'll be dead when they wake me up in the morning," he thought. "Little Bones and I."

He arched his neck and drew the pillows tighter and closer.

"This is easy," he thought. "It's easy. Why didn't Gilbert think of it?"

His brain felt as though it were floating away from him—out into the room…above him…around him. He watched himself, detached and calm.

"Why, I'm asleep," he thought. "I'm ony sleeping. That's all."

A soft belling sounded from faraway. But it was just a noise in his head which began to ring all through him as he pressed into the softness of the feathers.

He felt himself tighten—and gasp.

Someone came into the room.

"It's all right, Hook, don't worry," said a voice.

He turned violently.

A figure stood, black, in the doorway.

"I just wanted to say good night," it said.

Hooker drew a deep breath and shuddered, hard.

The person came near and sat down.

"Is there anything you're not—sure of, love, before you go to sleep?"

Hooker felt his burned hands being taken. He withdrew them and lay very still.

After a moment, the voice continued:

"A long, long time ago, my father died. That was your grandfather. He was only sick, of course, and he died in bed, and I wasn't there with him. I can remember that it made me sorry. I felt sorry for *him*. And I was sorry because he never said good-bye to me." There was a pause and some long breathing, and then, quietly, almost as though not really to Hooker at all, the voice went on: "I didn't forgive him for that. Not for a long time. In fact, I didn't forgive him until tonight."

There was another pause, and Hooker watched as the angle of the person's head changed and bent toward him. The chin was little and round. It was Rosetta, and she kissed him.

"But she has killed Gilbert," Hooker thought. "And someone should have to forgive *her*."

"All people don't die so desperately," she said. "There is a choice. Gilbert, you see, didn't know about that. He made so many mistakes, all through his life. He didn't know how to sort things out."

Hooker blinked and tried to see her face. She stroked his forehead now.

"But—there is nothing for you to be afraid of," she said finally. "Or to worry about." And then she rose. "Because I love you, and Daddy loves you. Iris loves you and"—"Don't say that my mother loves me,"

Hooker thought—"your mother loves you, too. All right?"

Hooker nodded, and then said, "Yes," into the dark.

"Good night," said Rosetta. "All the doors are open, dear, and I'll leave yours open, too. Especially. If there's anything you want, just call us. We're all here."

"We're not all here," Hooker thought.

Then she went away down the hall.

Hooker tried not to sleep. He wanted to remember what she had said to him. Perhaps she did not know she had lied to him. She couldn't have known. He had never heard her lie so well before.

And then he thought, "I'll ask her again in the morning. And if she says it again, I'll look at her. I'll see."

Little Bones stretched out hard beside him.

Hooker dreamed, far-off in the dark. It was quiet, there, and safe, and you didn't have anything difficult to know or anything baffling that you didn't know. Dying was so easy. Like this sleep, for instance, which you had just by turning over. Or like a killing, which, as it was with Rosetta, you did just by saying things, like—

Oh, well...

...like...

...well, like...

Oh, well.

Like that.

Chapter Twenty

In September there was an inquest.

Nicholas, Rosetta, Iris, and even Hooker had to testify. The Harrises were called and Mr. Parker, also, because they had stood with Gilbert on the terrace just prior to his suicide.

Everyone was very polite to the Winslows, as a family. Those who spoke to them lowered their voices. Hooker felt as though he must be on TV. They were all together in a large room, very much like a courtroom; some policemen and a coroner were with them, and a small, baldheaded little man who sat at a large table, alone, typing out the proceedings.

Hooker could not quite grasp that they were not in court, like Perry Mason, but only at a hearing, an inquest. Iris sat beside him, explaining things as they happened. Nicholas and Rosetta had testified and sat in front of them in captain's chairs, which had black leather across the backs.

"Mr. Clarke," someone said, addressing the coroner, "the decedent's brother is here. A minor."

"How old is he?"

"Eleven."

"Oh, well, then. That's fine. That's fine. Eleven.
Eleven. I was afraid you might mean a little three-year-
old, a four-year-old—or some little *child*."

"Hooker Winslow."

"Go on," said Iris, smiling. "You go now, an' I'll go
next. Just say what you like, but tell the truth."

Hooker walked forward to testify.

The old man, who was the coroner, looked at him
severely. He had a gray face and large, blue eyes.

"You will tell the truth, won't you?"

"Yes, sir."

"Very well, then."

Everyone seemed to wait.

The coroner said, "When did you last see your
brother, Hooker? Before the accident."

"On the terrace."

"When?"

"Just before."

"I see. Just before the accident—like your aunt and
your father."

"Two or three minutes before that, yes."

"What was he doing?"

"Talking."

"To whom, Hooker? Whom was he talking to?"

"My aunt. Aunt Rosetta." Instinctively he looked at
her. She did not look back. Her face was almost hidden
behind a veil, but he could tell that she did not look at
him from the angle of her head.

"Do you know what he was saying?"

"He gave her back her purse. She'd dropped it. I
think he said, 'Here is your purse.'"

"And then what happened?"

"He left, and some people danced again, and there was an explosion."

"Did you go to where the explosion was?"

"Yes."

"Where was it?"

"On the hill."

"At the golf club?"

"Yes."

"Did you see your brother?"

Hooker did not answer.

"Did you see Gilbert at the explosion?"

"Yes."

"He was dead?"

"Yes."

"Had you spoken to him that day?"

"No."

"The day before?"

"Yes."

"What did he say?"

Hooker looked at Iris. She smiled. He pretended to remember.

"He told me about going to school."

"Yes?"

"And he said I wouldn't like it."

"Anything else?"

"Yes."

Iris watched him carefully.

"What else?"

"About a poem he'd written..."

"Poem?"

"At school, and that it wasn't true about Janice Parker."

Everyone talked.

"What wasn't true about Janice Parker, Hooker?"

"I don't know," said Hooker. "He said it wasn't true about her, that's all. And he said, 'Do you believe me?' and I said—"

"What?"

"I said—"

Iris lifted her hands out of her lap.

"I said, 'Yes, I do…'"

Someone coughed.

"'believe you.' And I said so because I did."

The coroner said that was fine and called on Iris Browne to speak.

Hooker sat down and watched her. Before she had been nervous. Now she was not nervous at all. Hooker smiled. She smiled back.

Hooker thought, "Gilbert told her about the poem, too. And she believed him."

The questioning began.

"Miss Browne…"

Chapter Twenty-one

They got to the front door and waited.

Seeing them hesitate on the step in this uncertain fashion, any casual observer would have been under the impression that they did not belong there.

And for a moment, it seemed they did not.

However, Iris eventually became nervous, standing there that way, looking lost like that, and she advanced on the green door, as she might from inside to let someone in.

"Well, I'm going in," she said out loud, "and make tea."

Voices mumbled indistinctly, intending to convey interest, but no one really achieved the proper vocal proportions of an answer. So, Iris went in alone without further communication.

Finally, Rosetta said, "Well…that's that," and sighed and looked up at the opened door.

The hallway stood there, dark and empty, waiting to be filled.

Nicholas, his lips parted, his teeth set closed against each other and his eyelids drooping, shot an odd, hard look at his sister.

"This has been very easy for you, hasn't it?" he said.
She looked back at him but did not speak.

Hooker hardened like a person preparing to be hit.
It was not perceptible on his face, which remained
openly in repose, but inside the clamps had caught
fast.

After a pause, Rosetta said, "We're home, Nicholas.
Home, dear. Let's go inside."

Nicholas looked at her again, and seeing her exam-
ining the flower beds, her little round head turned to
one side, he coughed. She was so—enormously small,
he thought. She should be a dwarf. He recited to himself a prosaic description: "I watch her, and she seems
to be perpetually smiling in a crooked, secret way. She
is wearing flat-heeled shoes and tiny white gloves, and
as so often, nowadays, she is dressed as if she were still
a little girl—even though she's in her sixties..." The
words stopped composing themselves suddenly, and
Nicholas walked in. He was tired of prose. Tired of
thoughts. His son was dead.

But as the others watched him, they saw only his
splay-foot walk fill up the hall with energy and anger.
He did not remove his hat. His cane diggled to a stop
at his side, and he leaned into its angled support.

"I will have a glass of sherry," he said to Rosetta.

It was so unusual for him to say this in front of the
family that Hooker stared at him.

Rosetta walked in, put her purse, navy blue, on the
table beneath the mirror—in which were reflected a
dozen white-and-blue flowers from the cutting garden—and she gracefully removed one glove and
rearranged every single blossom that there was, all

twelve, and then took a handkerchief from her sleeve, dusted the top of the table—naturally, already quite clean—and finally blew her nose. All of this constituted one continuous and almost beautiful gesture, as though a butterfly had done it and then folded its wings.

Afterward she turned and stared at Nicholas.

Hooker went in, now, and stood beside the door to the living room. He watched his cats rising in turn to greet him with a yawn and a bow from the long, deep, chintzed-over sofa. Automatically he turned around to see if Rosetta had seen them, but she had not, this time.

Suddenly Nicholas went rigid. His mouth, already filled with saliva, opened and spoke from behind his yellow, even teeth, flecked with tobacco chips. The noise he made was not words, only syllables.

He said several noises, while his teeth closed over them in a series of expert spasms.

Rosetta butterflied forward.

"Come, now," she said, as calmly as could be, to Nicholas. "I will take your things, dear. You're just having a coughing fit."

Nicholas continued to cough but only lightly.

"That's all right, dear," said Rosetta, stripping the overcoat from his stony figure. "We'll all stay down stairs for a while."

She shot a look at Hooker.

"Help me with your father's things," she said.

Hooker came over and took away the cane, the black homburg hat, the gray-black overcoat, the useless rubbers, and the gloves.

Rosetta applied a little physical pressure on her brother's shoulder. She reached away up and touched him, very gently.

"Oh, dear," she said. "Now come along in."

They walked into length after length of room—daylit, where the cats were—and Nicholas said, "I don't know. I don't know."

"Yes," said Rosetta. "Poor love. Of course."

"What is being done?" Nicholas said, rummaging for his cigarettes.

"Everything," said Rosetta. Already she was rearranging the ash trays all around the room. She stopped and pulled one of the rugs straight with the flat heel of her little shoe. "Then the phone will probably start to ring."

"But—not to know what people really think..." Nicholas began.

"Nick. I don't want to know. I don't want to hear any more about it. We did our duty. We went. We sat there. We answered all the questions. Even Hooker. Even Iris. Now it's all over."

Nicholas lighted his cigarette with a wooden match.

"Don't throw it on the floor, dear."

Nicholas let the match burn on toward his finger ends.

"I feel so hypocritical," he said.

"Well, you're not," said Rosetta. "Dear!"

The match went out, burning his thumb very slightly.

"But did I say the right things?"

"And more," said Rosetta. "Much more. We were all quite, quite honest."

Somewhere, faraway upstairs, they could hear the ominous sound of Jessica walking.

"Who's up there?"

"Dear!" Rosetta stared. "Jessica."

Nicholas set his teeth again in an automatic gesture of nervous apprehension.

"Did you see the way everyone stared at me?"

"Now, Nicholas."

"'That's his father'…'That *was* his father!' As if *I'd* killed my*self!*"

"Well…"

"In the name of *God!*"

Hooker leaned into the room without listening.

"Please, I'd like to go out," he said.

"Well, you won't," said Nicholas. "Not now. Not all day."

Iris came into the room, wheeling the tea wagon filled with cups, bottles, glasses, spoons, a teapot, and a creamer.

"Miss Winslow, I hear walking," she said.

"I know," said Nicholas. "So did we."

"Is one of us going to go up or what, then?"

"We shall wait."

"But you know it isn't right. She's not to be up yet. Doctor gave her a sedative and all. I mean—"

Nicholas looked at Rosetta, but Rosetta was busy settling herself on the sofa.

"Well, maybe then—you'd better go up."

Rosetta's eyes rose in Nicholas' direction.

"Nicholas! Leave Jessie alone."

"Go up, Iris."

"Yes, sir."

Iris was still wearing her black hat with the little plume. She walked out of the room and slowly mounted the stairs.

Nicholas regarded the bottles, selected one, and poured himself a glass of sherry. Rosetta watched him carefully.

"I shall have whiskey," she said.

"I thought you were having tea," said Nicholas.

Rosetta did not reply.

Nicholas walked toward one of the long windows, to look into the garden.

"It's cold in here," he said. "And that damned chamber was appallingly hot. They must have had every furnace in creation turned on in there."

Rosetta smiled.

Hooker handed her the bottle of whiskey and a glass, and started back toward the doorway.

"Dear!" said Rosetta. "Don't leave me with the bottle, Hooker!"

Nicholas said, "Why not?" and laughed drily.

Rosetta rose and replaced the bottle on the wagon. She poured water into her glass.

Hooker wanted to hear what was happening upstairs. There were voices, now.

He picked at his cuticles, standing hidden in his old place among the drapes, every once in a while looking out at the hall and then standing very still again, waiting.

"Why should it bother one so, about those people staring?"

"No reason, dear. None. It's just natural, that's all. You'll feel it now, and then you'll forget it," said

Rosetta. Now she settled back, waiting for Iris to come downstairs. She straightened the line of her hair netting. "I can only think of them as people far too—" She fumbled for some word or other, left it out, and said, "As people I'd never dream of making friends with. Nor would you. They have perverted curiosity, that's all."

"But he did kill himself," said Nicholas, as though that were the hidden clue as to what they should all be thinking. "One of us has killed himself."

Rosetta immediately started talking, very quickly.

"Now, dear! You know that he was the kind of boy who always gave out a false picture to strangers," she said. "And you know what I mean." She made a face toward Hooker, indicating that the conversation should end.

Upstairs the voices rose in a crisis.

Hooker started forward but fell back.

"What the hell are they doing?" said Nicholas.

"Probably Iris is trying to quiet her down."

"It's like having a bloody gun at your head all the time."

"Nicholas!"

They became quite silent.

Nicholas looked at Rosetta expectantly, but she was still busy with her hair pins, gazing into her lap, where a pile of them lay, shiny and sun-speckled. Her fingers moved with brilliant efficiency—ringless and plain and quick.

Another wave of sounds descended.

Nicholas obviously felt ringed in by alternate loops of frustration and apathy. He wanted to say something to Rosetta, to accuse her. Or to forgive her. But he did not do either. He made motions with his hands instead.

"I can't do anything, when something's wrong like this," he said. "I can't even move."

Rosetta went on being quiet. She sipped from her whiskey glass and brushed at the little white hairs that had fallen onto her shoulders.

Then Nicholas sat down.

The three of them were quite still for a moment, and Nicholas sighed.

Hooker watched his father and shuffled the curtain by the doorway, where he continued to stand. Gilbert had killed himself. And had been cremated.

In a deepening silence, listening to Jessica and Iris, they were all really thinking of Gilbert in the fire—in the fires—of his suicide and of his cremation.... And of the coroner and of the inquest and its verdict: "Death by his own hand."

Among the folds of velvet, Hooker was trying not to think about the fires.

"How do they know you're dead?" he thought. "I mean, he was dead, but how do they *know*? What if he wasn't? What'd happen? He might yell—might even get up and pound at the door of the furnace—but they'd never hear him with all that noise."

He thought of the crackling roar that had burned his own hands. And of the firemen. Why had they put out one fire only to light another?

Then he thought about boxes.

What if you woke up in a coffin? What would happen to you? You'd pound on the lid. But could you even move your arms? How could you get into a proper pounding position?

Unconsciously now he folded up each hand tightly. Then he made small, elbow-drive gestures into the curtains.

"Stop that," said Nicholas.

Hooker relaxed.

What if you were in a grave?

What if you got the lid up? Then the earth would be there, and it would fall, all lumpy and wetted, into your mouth. You'd choke with it. You wouldn't be able to breathe.

There was another noise, just then, faraway, enclosed, somewhere upstairs and beyond the walls.

The three heads turned again to listen.

"I'm sure," thought Hooker, "that you could never, never no matter what you did—get out."

He stood very still and listened—as they all did.

Chapter Twenty-two

Hooker wandered.

It was four o'clock, the afternoon of the inquest.

Rosetta was asleep on the couch in her office. Her black dress, which very carefully reached to her knees, was smooth, and her hands were in repose, like little dead birds in her lap. Her feet, shoeless, stuck straight up into the air.

Hooker stood in the doorway and watched her frankly.

Rosetta's face was white and round, and her hair made circular designs on the pillow beneath her head. Her eyelids were gray. A magazine, which had been across her face, had fallen to the floor, and Hooker felt an impulse to pick it up and replace it—but he did not stir.

The room was filled with an oldness that was more than just the age itself of the furniture. It was old in the air that was there—old in the very dimness that was constant in the corners, old in the quality of remembrance that Rosetta had breathed upon the surface of each and every article within its bounds.

There were shelves of careful photographs—gray and brown and black and white, with tinted faces and rose-pink hands, each figure balanced on the edge of eternity forever, smiling and poised and dead.

Hooker shot a look at his aunt and moved in, to the center of the room.

It was intensely cool.

The smell of soap came to him, undeniably clean and unmitigated. There was no complication of odors in Rosetta's office, as there might be in the rest of the house. The smell was simply that of cleanliness.

Hooker touched the fingers of one hand to those of the other, behind his back. He leaned across the table top toward some of the photographs.

There were the faces. There was his history, and he could touch it.

In a row were all the men—grandfathers...uncles... fathers...and sons. Brothers. Cousins...nephews... male relations of every description at every possible age. There was his own great-grandfather, bearded, cold, responsible for future generations. There, too, was Grandfather Winslow, large, impossibly young, and striking in a suit and vest, fingering his golden watch chain, which stretched, expensively resplendent, across the ample fact of his belly. He was trying, it seemed, very hard to impress on posterity the fact that life for him was something strict and moral. Yet, in his eyes, he failed to do so. There was something to witness otherwise, for they attested to the pain of life, and they had obviously known the undiluted pleasures of food and wife and great financial prosperity. His mouth was a little grim, however, and it turned away from what one could not avoid concluding was its natural inclination—to smile. His teeth, apparently, constantly grated against each other—rather like Nicholas' teeth—and his jawbone could be seen through the skin, tight and unnatural. But it was a face, once beheld, never to be forgotten. In it were all the secrets of tragedy and all the frankness of uncomplicated honesty. It was the face of someone greatly loved. A face revered in public for its strength—but caressed in private for its weakness.

Hooker had never met him.

The memory of him was ancient.

And there he was.

Rosetta spoke but only from her sleep. Hooker shrank back and eyed her carefully. Her eyelids broadened tightly, as though beneath them she had come awake. Her face fell back toward its lines of paralysis, like an army retreating to its trenches. But she did not otherwise stir.

Gulliver wandered into the room through the open door. He had a doglike face, large white teeth, and Hitler's moustache on a black-and-white countenance. He chirruped inquisitively and came, with an oversized, stumbling gait, toward Hooker.

He was swept from the floor and enclosed, for the sake of silence.

Then Hooker looked at the remaining photographs.

There were some of the town as it used to be—this quiet part of the town where they were living now and had lived then. Where, it seemed to Hooker, they had lived forever.

Passing down the brick sidewalks, the men in the photographs wore ties to work all summer long and came home past the old lawns that still, in the present, smelled of petunia plants, mock orange blossoms, and rubber hoses that sprinkled the grass with water long forgotten. Hooker could see that the men called out to each other—names unknown, greetings now meaningless and dead—and he could see that there was a different code of ethics and behavior, different to the one he knew on the street today. The women who accompanied the men in the photographs touched, from a delicately possessive distance, the poplin arms of their husbands. Not one of them spoke. Not one of them looked directly into the lens of the camera. He perceived that they were quiet and different. They seemed contented, pleased.

They stood in front of, or passed by, the old houses—including, Hooker saw, the Harrises' house—which were partly hidden by old trees and set apart by fences and hedges or by the remarkable length of their lawns, back from the street. These lawns were empty, except where occasionally a child had left an old-fashioned bicycle spilled, white and gleaming, on the grass. Or where late-working gardeners were still tardily busy, buzzing lazily with rackety, newfangled lawn mowers. It seemed that the time of day was always close to sundown, in these photographs, for the shadows everywhere were long and menacing.

In one of this group of pictures, a small knot of shirt-sleeved men, all of them wearing boater hats, bow ties, and tight, high-waisted trousers, stood in the sunlight at the foot of a private walk and looked off, talking in smiles to each other, into a deep garden where dogs, prostrated by the heat, lay stretched out with their noses in the shade, and to where, sitting seemingly for some "occasion," cats could be seen staring from the open windows of a house.

Among this group of young men, Hooker perceived John Harris, smiling, and the muted face of his father. Young. Nicholas. Young.

On the shelf below, in photoed gardens, again toward the dark side of an evening, some children lingered under their favorite trees or sat on quiet swings, singing wordless children's songs. Or they lay in dreams along the cool white railings of the porches and verandahs of their houses, recognizable to Hooker as those just down the street. These picture children were dressed in shady, off-white costumes, and they looked like dusty moths, hovering, yet stilled forever, at the edge of the dark.

He could see, among the faces there, the childhood likenesses of several relatives, all of them Winslows— and pictured again and again was the rounded, worried stare of Aunt Rosetta. She was dressed in the triangular fashion of the time, and her hats were round and ribboned. Her hands were always resting—in waiting, patient. An incredible intelligence, some sort of superiority, set her visage apart from every other. She was beautiful and odd—and touching. But Hooker knew that it was senseless to say so, and he was wise enough to know that it was a sad aloofness that made it so. He gazed back at her, now, on her sofa.

Was it possible? Had she ever let anything complimentary or flattering be said?

He thought not. There was, certainly, nothing happy you could say to her now. She did not want to be told anything. She just wanted to be safe, and that meant cold and sure and true and touchless. Was it this that had made that moment with Gilbert so impossible to avoid?

Hooker held Gulliver closer to his chest.

He breathed deeply. He wanted to wake Rosetta up. He wanted, finally, to ask her questions about love...about John Harris...about her father...but when he looked at her again, he knew that her determined silence could never be broken. Her opinion of everything had been firmly decided, long ago, some time in the olden days, the day before her photographs, when she had been a child—perhaps afraid, as he was, of growing up. Of being the next in line.

Back in the long dark hall, Hooker set Gulliver down on the floor and watched the small tip of white on the lanky tail going away into shadow, as the cat ambled off toward another part of the house.

Everywhere it was quiet.

He pushed his left forefinger along the old green wallpaper and followed it with little steps until it jammed against the edge of the library door.

He saw Gilbert.

He pushed open the big oak door. A smell of dampness, leather, and tobacco pushed back at him, holding him still. The room was dimmed out because the long, translucent, shade-of-ivory curtains were drawn across the windows. Wasn't Gilbert lying on the sofa?

His shoes, like Rosetta's, had been removed, but instead of being neatly arranged nearby as hers had been, they were thrown to the opposite end of the room, where they lay, soles upward. Hooker could smell feet and perspiration. He looked, casually aware of all the implications of the scene—and then remembered.

He wondered what would happen next.

Why had Gilbert had to lie there? He wasn't lazy—not in his mind. In his body, he was, but that was force of habit more than anything else. Rosetta had said so. She had said it all the time. With his thoughts, Gilbert had moved around in such enormous sentences and active arguments that anyone who listened was terrified, because the thoughts were always angry and pointed and sometimes true. It was impossible, most often, to quiet him down at all, and yet he always, forever, complained that no one listened to him or gave him a chance to speak. He was desperate for words—for a voice—to make noises. Someone had to pay attention. Iris was his only constant audience. And Hooker. Now. In his mind.

Sometimes, if he had lost a listener in one room, Gilbert would simply get up, walk away talking and continue the edict somewhere, to other unlistening ears. Many times he had cornered Hooker and absolutely made him listen, through sheer force of volume. Their mother was always saying that he should have been a lawyer or a politician, that he argued well. She was proud of the way he spoke. At least, she had been. Once.

Automatically, as he thought of his mother, Hooker glanced up at the ceiling. She would be resting now.

How full this house could be of silence.

He liked it when it was quiet this way. It was good to feel that no one really knew he was there, except Iris, who by now would probably be asleep, too, in the kitchen.

He looked back at Gil's room, and thought about the photographs in Rosetta's office. Grandfathers... fathers and sons. Face patterns. The nose, the wide, high forehead. The bigness and the weight.

Hooker advanced into the room.

The remembered smell of wine and feet and sweat made him feel dizzy and odd and full. The sweet smells seemed out of context in the dry and musty atmosphere of the library, mingled with his brother's voice. It looked as if someone had left Gil there, spilled, without arrangement, on the sofa. But it was only an old blanket and a pillow.

Beside them, on the floor, close now to where Hooker stood, were the papers Gil had been writing on earlier in the week. It had been a habit of Gil's, when cloistered with his bottle of wine, to write these endless lists. Lists of dates and lists of places. Lists of hockey stars, movie stars, historical figures. Lists of battles, generals, victories. Lists of poets, playwrights, authors. Lists of occasions, real and imaginary—occasions such as birthdays, anniversaries, public holidays. Timetables.

All of these, together with sharp male faces drawn in the left profile, covered an endless array of sheets of paper.

Hooker read the one on top, moving a broken pencil stub to see what was written.

"Gilbert Hugo Winslow," he read, "1940-1964. Rest in Peace without remembrance."

"...the One remains, the many change and pass;
Heaven's light forever shines, Earth's shadows fly;

251

Life, like a dome of many-coloured glass,
Stains the white radiance of Eternity,
Until Death tramples it to fragments.—Die,
    If thou wouldst be with that which thou dost
seek!
    Follow where all is fled!"

Hooker thought of Rosetta's photographs—of all
the dead.

"Follow where all is fled.
Follow.
Follow Gil. H. Winslow—you whitewashed
                            son of a bitch,
Follow in peace where all is...
Ding-dong the cat is dead which old cat the kid's
old cat ding dong the wicked old cat is...
Buy the kid a dog!

R.I.Pee!"
And then...
    "6:00 P.M.: Scare shit out of Nick.
    6:30 P.M.: Wake up Mother.
    sometime-evening? a.m.? p.m.? Sleep!
    Hooker finally hooked (hah-hah!)
    2:00 A.M.: Finish first bottle R.
        Start N. two."

Next came a primitive artistic attempt at someone's
likeness, badly out of perspective, and finally, these
words:

"It is Fear, oh Little Hunter—it is Fear.
Rudyard Kipling—R.I.Pee."

Hooker folded the paper and carried it away.

He replaced, however, before he withdrew, the broken pencil stub and stood for a moment gazing at the rows and rows of books:

The Wind in the Willows... Clausewitz on War... Chums '39... Chums '40... Chums '41... The Duke...

In the kitchen, Iris rested her arms on the table and gazed, very tired, from the window into the dusty summer yard.

She had wept, sitting all alone, for an hour, and now was exhausted.

"If only that baby had lived," she thought, "I'd have something more to do."

But she only rested.

Hooker passed into the open width of the entrance hall.

There he saw Nicholas in the living room, still dressed in the dark, heavy suit he had worn to the inquest.

He was absolutely still. He sat gazing, awake, from staring eyes, into the lengthy garden beyond the farthest windows of the room at the lawn.

Hooker tiptoed further off, toward the stairs, afraid to be seen or heard.

On the table, Rosetta's flowers had lifted their heads higher, struggling to find breathing space between the layers of heat.

Nicholas coughed.

"Is that you?" he said. He did not turn. There was something peculiar about the tilt of his head. It was held impeccably upright, as though he had just put it on a stick and raised it up from the depths of the chair he sat in.

"You're not to come in," he said.

Hooker listened for the voice again. It was quiet, constricted, horrified.

"Go back...get back to your room. You shouldn't be down here."

He turned.

Hooker stepped away.

He saw that his father was physically afraid.

Nick's face had taken on a cast of color from the green walls, and it was set with lines Hooker had never seen there before—lines that looked like painful chisel cuts. His eyes, which were almost loosened from their sockets, were laced red, yellow, instead of white—and jet black where they should have been blue.

Gradually, the features, lines, and planes became assembled once again and took on the appearances that Hooker knew.

"Are you there?" said Nicholas.

"Yes, Father."

"Who?"

"Hooker, Father."

Nick returned his head statically to its former position, eyes forward, a gradual relaxation rippling down the taut bulk of his neck.

There was a long moment filled up with Hooker standing still and with a sigh from Nicholas.

"You're thinking something that isn't true," he said.

Hooker was quiet.

"And I warn you—"

The sentence remained there unfinished.

"Come here."

Hooker went nearer. He stood at the back of his father's chair.

"Right here."

Hooker went around to the front and stood with his back to the light.

"Can you see me?" said Nicholas.

Hooker nodded. "Yes."

"What do you see?"

"You're crying."

"Yes."

Hooker fumbled, nervously embarrassed.

"Is there anything I can do for you?" he asked.

"No."

They were silent again.

Nicholas took out a cigarette package and undid the wrappings clumsily. The cellophane crunkled like machine-gun fire, and he could not manage to break the revenue stamp without tearing the box itself. After lighting his cigarette, he began the inevitable fiddling with the match.

Hooker's feet were hot in his running shoes. He felt as if they were rotting. He coughed lightly. Nick's eye's flew out at him sharply.

"What's the matter?" his father said.

It was another ridiculous question. Hooker's mind clamped in a seizure. He could not produce any coherent thought by which to answer or escape. He merely looked back at his father with a dumbness that to Nicholas was typical and calculated.

"*Cat* got your tongue?" he said. It was one of his answers to catastrophe. Humor. Hooker remembered the picture of a naked man lying dead in the ruins of a fire. His father had given this newspaper photograph a glance and had remarked, "What a strange place for him to sunbathe!"—after which he had laughed, very lightly.

Now Nicholas said, "Did you understand the inquest?"

"Yes."

"You understood the questions you were asked?"

Nick's voice floated on a single note, like a boat on oily water—slick and full of phlegmy depths.

"Yes."

"Unh-hunh. What did you think of the verdict?" The curious tone did not change.

Hooker's mind numbed over.

"Hooker?"

"Sir?"

"What did you think of the verdict? Was it just?"

"Yes, sir."

Pause.

"I see. Have you been up to see your mother?"

Nicholas regarded the match end.

"No."

"Are you going to?"

He inserted the match end under a finger nail.

"I thought we weren't supposed to."

"We aren't." He coughed. "I just wondered if you had."

"No…I haven't."

Another pause ensued. A little more adrenalin had been fired in each of them. Nick's stomach burned. He slitted his eyes and spoke carefully, touching the quick, reaching gently, delicately, far under his nail.

"Just how much about everything do you know by now?" he asked.

Hooker was afraid.

"Gilbert was—"

"I don't mean that."

"Don't make me afraid," Hooker wanted to say. "Don't make me so afraid."

Aloud, he was speechless. He breathed in.

"You're eleven," said Nicholas.

"Yes. Almost twelve."

"Eleven. You're eleven." Nicholas was confused. "Really, are you eleven?" It was an absolute question for a change, one that needed answering without a smile.

"Yes. I'm eleven. That was my last birthday. Eleven."

"Unh-hunh." Nicholas looked at the end of the match, rolling it lightly between his fingers.

After a moment, he said carefully, "I'm sorry about your summer. It's completely ruined. Your—mother. Your brother. All this."

"It's all right."

Nick's foot tapped. He fished around quietly, apparently trying to find some words, some way to say something. And then he said, with a catch in his throat, "Are you—uh—satisfied that you know all about what happened to Gilbert?"

"He killed himself," said Hooker.

Nick's eyes flickered hopelessly to one side.

"We know that, Hooker. But do you really *understand*? Why, for instance."

The implication, of course, was that Hooker did not—simply could not be expected to know anything—and so he began to breathe in a peculiar fashion. He felt blamed, in some way. He was slightly aware that his father needed his answer for some purpose.

The oily waters smeared.

"Your brother was not at all like other people. Did you know that?"

"No." Hooker knew that the right answer was "Yes."

The gulf widened.

Now, apparently, his father changed the subject.

"I notice that you have no friends," he said. He waited for an answer, and then he did not wait. Neither did he wait to give an explanation.

"Where is it you go when you're alone?"

The tone was casual.

"Off..." said Hooker. "I walk."

"And you're alone?"

"Sometimes..."

Nick's eyes lifted.

"One of the animals—Gulliver...Little Bones..." said Hooker, "usually goes...."

"And where do these walks—occur?"

Hooker did not want to say where.

"Different places."

"In the woods?"

"Yes."

"In those fields back there—our fields?"

"Yes."

"Down in the town?"

"Once in a while."

"In the park?"

"What park?"

Nicholas maintained the quiet approach.

"*The* park. The park—the *park*." He made a circular gesture.

"No," said Hooker.

"You've been to the zoo?"

"Well…yes."

"That's where I mean, then. There. That park."

"Yes. I've been there."

"Did you ever go anywhere with Iris?"

"Yes. Downtown."

"Any other place? Other places?"

Hooker remembered, carefully.

"Once or twice."

"What happened?"

"We met a friend of hers."

"Who?"

"Alberta."

Nicholas was quiet.

Hooker added, "Perkins."

Nicholas puffed on his cigarette and held on to the edges of the chair he sat in.

The air itself moved with it now—elastic and hot and precarious. The idea that something was about to be totally amiss and go wrong.

"Would you ever let me come with you?"

Hooker went white. There it was. The question. Just as he had known it had to be there. He felt old and sick.

"No," he said.

He heard the sound of it—"no" and "no" and "no"—inside.

Nicholas sighed.

He would not talk to anyone anymore. He could not make anyone listen to him. All the right words remained in his mind, where he inserted them between the phrases he said aloud. He would not speak anymore. He would not talk to anyone.

At last, he put down the match.

"I'm afraid..." ("Of how quiet we are.")

Then he stubbed his cigarette and moved slightly in his chair.

The movement was always a signal that the conversation was drawing to a close. But Nicholas himself was not aware of that. He did not knowingly do it conclusively.

"When you grow up," said Nicholas, "and you have a child of your own..."

Now he had thrown away the oars and was drifting away across a vast expanse of water, into fog....

("When you realize the things you have to face—when you see your children growing away from life, when nothing you say means anything to anyone anymore, and you are crying out "help" or "beware" or "caution," and no one pays attention—then...then...then, it will be different, Hooker. When there is sex and perfidy and frustration and meanness—everywhere—to trap you...")

Hooker watched him.

"Can I get you anything?" he asked.

Nicholas allowed the slightest of rueful smiles to

impress his features and then go.

There was a real sadness in him, now—the boat had drifted so far from the shore, where not even the shoals of chance could be of any danger...

"I think I'll sit here for a while," he said very quietly.

Hooker stared, but Nicholas did not elaborate.

As Hooker left the room, Nicholas remarked, inside his mind, that it was pointless, utterly pointless, to try to be all things to all men. And then he slept.

Jessica's room was sunlit when Hooker went in.

She herself was sitting, asleep, in her chair, and she was dressed in the blue robe. Her feet, encased in black shoes, could just be seen under the edge of a knitted covering. Her hands, in her lap, were folded upon the pages of an open book.

Hooker watched her stealthily and jiggered the door to a close, deftly and with near silence. The click was followed by the hollow sound of motionless air, enclosed.

Hooker slipped his shoes off by the heel and barefooted it across to the bed.

He stood there, quiet, with his fingers splayed open upon the coverlet. He began to breathe more easily. In the living room, with his father, he had nearly suffocated with fear and confusion.

He lay down.

From the bed, looking sideways, he regarded his mother as she sat in her chair. He could see her very distinctly, across the room, even though he was drowsy and the rest of his body very nearly slept. He blinked his eyes to clear them of the shimmer from light, which fell on them from the windows across the room. Jessica seemed like a figure cut from ice, in the process of being melted.

He looked at her face.

She was so pale, and there was perspiration on her forehead. Her mouth had a hard, unfortunate look. It looked as though the lips were trying to invert and disappear. She looked very much like one who is afraid to speak, because she might lose something precious that was hidden under her tongue. The secret of retreat.

Hooker lay still.

Jessie's eyes were enclosed in shade-of-violet lids without any veins in them—like lids of melted, pure, and unmarked marble—while the rest of her face was of a plastery texture, ready to unseam and come away in pieces.

But for all its hardness and mystery, his mother's face was sad to him and beautiful. Hooker did not quite understand this, but on her face there was marked the presence of thwarted peace. Jessie had almost found her haven, when, violently, they had pulled her back from its door.

"My mother wants to be good," Hooker thought. "And perhaps Gilbert wanted to be good, too."

In his mind there was a long silence. And then...

He wondered if that was what made them crazy.

The afternoon began to wear itself away beyond the windows. A breeze seriously trifled with the leaves and soon with whole branches of the trees. It became almost cool, although indoors, it was not immediately perceptible.

Hooker watched his mother.

One little fly buzzed in a loud panic against the screen.

Death.

Hooker looked long and hard at Jessica.

He saw her arms and the chewed silver bracelets. He saw the thinness of her wrists.

He saw her hands, resting on the little book, an old notebook of poetry and other writings which she cherished privately. And he remembered.

Once, Hooker had seen inside this book, and just before he slept, now, the words he had seen then came into his mind.

His mother had put down in her funny, wavering handwriting:

> "If thou hast a fearful thought,
> Share it no with a weakling.
> Whisper it to thy saddle-bow
> And ride forth singing."

"Written by the king (Alfred), she had written, 849-901 A.D."

Hooker looked one last time at Jessie's face.

He had a fearful thought.

The fly now ceased to buzz and bang, and Hooker slept.

Epilogue

Waiting in the stable, the boy and the cat at last were answered.

"Hook!"

It was beginning.

Hooker drew the box close and opened it. He lifted the revolver up into view before his eyes, and it gleamed for him, oiled and ready, in his grasp. He inserted six bullets and placed six more, ready, on the tattered purple silk. He drew a sighting on the place that led into the garden from the porch. To do this, it was necessary to use both hands.

Iris approached the porch door.

"Hook!"

She disappeared from behind the screen, going back inside the house.

Hooker heard their voices, Rosetta and Iris, and then he heard one approach.

Rosetta.

"Get Mr. Winslow."

She stood beyond the solidified haze of metal and hugged her arms inside her dressing gown.

"I'm sure it's nothing to worry about," she yawned.

She called him.

"Hooker?"

Jessica appeared at her window.

"What is it?"

"Hooker."

"What?"

"Hooker is not in his room, that's all. Iris is concerned."

This conversation happened without confrontation. Rosetta stayed beyond the screen, and Jessie, seated in her chair by the window, made no effort to lean out or to look down. Behind their separate veils, of metal and of cloth, they each showed dim and featureless, wrapped in the lumpy shapes of robes and sleepiness.

"Look under the porch," said Jessica.

"Good heavens! Under the porch?"

"Children are always under the porch, Rosetta."

"Nonsense."

"They are. They are. They are, Rose. I was."

Rosetta did not reply.

Nicholas arrived, like an official at an event. Brushing past his sister, he came outside, and she, all at once thrown into the light, was revealed like a figure suddenly brought into focus on a screen. From the way she stood, hanging back, she seemed to resent the daylight's merciless revelation of herself in night attire. She grimaced.

Nicholas, already in midsentence, spoke out loud: "...not in his room," he said. "Then he's probably only gone for a walk. Good God, do we have to jump every time he decides to go for a walk?"

"Now, dear. It's seven thirty in the morning."

"What difference does that make?"

"Well…it's not like him. That's what."

Nicholas kicked at a stone with his slippered toes. He made a noise of disapproval but did not speak.

Rosetta hunched her shoulders. She seemed to be cold.

"Iris called him. He's not in the stable." She even sounded cold.

The other voice joined them.

"Good morning, Nicky."

Nicholas looked back at Rosetta with a question.

Rosetta shrugged and gestured above their heads.

Nicholas glanced up.

"Good morning, Jessie," he said.

"Look under the porch. Children are always under the porch. I was."

"Now, Jess…"

Jessica became violently petulant.

"Oh, Nicky. If you won't look and Rosetta won't," she said, "then I will!"

Her figure rose and disappeared beyond the curtains. Nicholas searched his sister's face for an escape from what he was certain was an impending crisis.

"Let her come down," said Rosetta. "It can't do any harm. Just ignore her being upset."

By now they were both standing in the yard. Nicholas lighted a cigarette. They waited silently, more intent, it seemed, upon the arrival of Jessica than on the finding of Hooker.

At last, Jessie got there, dressed still in the blue robe.

The sun turned everything extemely bright.

"Did you look?" she asked.

"Not yet, dear."

"Good. Then I will."

"I'll get some coffee," said Rosetta, and went back inside.

Hooker's parents were alone, now, in their back yard, waiting among the shrubs and the dust for their son.

Jessie, small and looking like a miniature painting of a queen, came down onto the dead and dying grass and got a bamboo rod from one of the flower beds, where it had held up a withered dahlia. She went over and poked this rod under the porch.

"Hookie! Hookie!" she cried. "Come, dear, come, dear—come out! Come out! Come out!"

It was the first time in months that she had called him.

There was no response.

"That's funny," said Jessie, straightening. "He's not there."

"We'll find him," said Nicholas.

"I ran away once," said Jessie, folding over her blue robe.

"Unh-hunh."

"I did!" She thought he did not believe her. "I went to Port Hope. With Jerome, my brother."

"Port Hope?"

"Yes. That's where I went. Hah. I took a little suit-case full of doll's clothes..." She smiled. "But I forgot to take the doll."

She laughed.

"Who brought you back?" Nicholas asked.

"My father." Her voice lowered. "He was very fond

of me, then."

"How old were you?"

"Oh, my goodness! I guess I was seven! Didn't you ever run away?"

Jessie laughed lightly now, almost inaudibly, and began to walk around the garden, using the bamboo rod as a walking stick.

"When St. Theresa was a little girl," she said, ignoring the fact that her husband had not answered her question, "about eight, I think, she ran off with *her* brother to become a sainted martyr of the Church. They were going all the way to Africa. I think it was Morocco. I've just read about it, you know."

She paused beside a lilac tree and held out her hand toward it. She spoke over her shoulder at Nick.

"Did I ever tell you about the time she threw the holy water at the devil, and he went away? St. Theresa—"

"No."

"In church." Jessie began to speak methodically, running leaves through her fingers as she talked: "She was in church. Yes? I think she was alone. And in came the devil. She was praying, you see, and he wanted to tempt her—anything to stop a prayer!"

Nick sighed and lighted another cigarette.

"St. Theresa took up some holy water and told him to go away. When she threw it in his direction, he disappeared. He did! In a puff of smoke. It was a miracle." She gazed at her feet. "Of course, she treats it very lightly in her book, as though it happened every day—but she was modest. It *was* a miracle, because the devil never came back."

There was a pause, in which Jessica stared with an odd smile at her husband.

Then, she let go of the branch, which swayed up and away from her, and she turned and walked one step toward the next tree.

"Gilbert…"

Nicholas watched her, listening.

"…is dead."

Nick shifted a little, staring at her carefully.

"Wasn't this a lovely garden," she said, "with all the trees in bloom?"

"Yes."

"Do you remember, dear? The little azalea trees and these lilacs and the syringa bush?"

"Syringa bush?"

"The mock orange, dear. For our wedding. It was planted for our wedding. By your father. Or was it by Rosetta? Your father died, didn't he? Yes. And all those lovely lilies-of-the-valley…"

Nicholas and Jessica both stared at the ground.

Rosetta returned with their coffee on a tray.

"Here," she said, handing it around.

"What's that?" said Jessica.

"Coffee, dear."

"No. No. That noise."

"What noise?"

"That noise. Click. Click."

"I don't hear anything, dear."

"Well, stop talking…"

Rosetta silenced herself and shaded her eyes with her free hand.

Nicholas sat down on the porch step, smoking and

drinking his coffee.

Jessica turned her head to one side.

"There. You hear that?"

Rosetta stared at the open bale door and at the dark interior of the stable loft beyond. She shivered. "Oh, my God!"

Hooker fired.

Nicholas and Jessie jerked their heads from the shock of the sound, and opened their eyes on the sight of Rosetta kneeling on the ground.

She seemed to have spilt her coffee, because she was desperately kneading, with both hands, at the front of her robe. Her cup had fallen to one side.

Nicholas began to rise.

The noise came again, violent and loud.

Nicholas fell back. On the step, his foot caught in the space between the boards.

Jessica behaved with wonderment. She waved her arms.

"What it it? What is it?" she asked. "Is there a storm? I—"

She had seen the dust rising at their feet.

"There must be a storm somehow. Rosetta? Rose…?"

Suddenly, Rosetta fell forward with the gesture of a Japanese Samurai who has committed hari-kari. She was watching Hooker all the way down. She was dead. Her back was crimson.

Nicholas tried once more to rise.

The sun became hidden, still and cool.

A third bang joined the others, jarring against the walls and fences, echoing sharply in their baffled ears.

Nicholas screamed. Beyond his deafness, he cried out:

"Run. Run. Run. Run. Run. Run. Run."

Iris came through the kitchen. She got as far as the porch.

"Run. Run. Oh, Jesus. Run."

Jessica looked at Rosetta, down in the dust and grass, and at her husband on the steps, and she turned, aware at last of what might be happening, toward the stable and the open door. Her face bore the expression of a child who has been lied to in a moment of crisis.

The gun was fired once more.

A noise, like the beating of clumsy wings, approached Jess through the lilac leaves, and she was struck, she thought, by a hand across the heart. She summoned her voice, but it would not come. She called it again, and it struggled, faraway in her mind, to obey her until it aimlessly wandered, lost, into silence.

Nicholas, on the step, received a second bullet, which he put his hand against before it broke through the flesh of his face and into his brain. He was thrown back into violent stillness.

Jessie, falling, kept her eyes upon the sky and on the images of leaves, falling away from her, up, in the wrong direction. At last the incredible blueness opened widely above her, and she saw her own hands falling, darker and darker, covering, faster and faster, nearer and nearer until, at the end, she felt them close upon her mouth in a gesture of amazed release.

It became so quiet that even Iris, running forward, could hear the final hiss of Nicholas' cigarette as it fell from his fingers into the coffee cup at the end of his extended arm.

She began to reach out with her voice.

She had run out the door, crossing Nicholas where he lay on the step, and now she raced toward the barn.

She reached the top of the ladder.

"Hookie?"

He did not stir.

Iris crawled, unaware of the sharp points of straw in her knees, and in this way, on all fours, she approached him. It did not occur to her, now, that he might shoot her. She just looked at him.

"Hook?"

She reached the gun out of his hands.

"There, honey," she said. "There now. There. There now. There you are. There."

He accepted her embrace.

"You're all right now," said Iris. "You've done it. It's over."

She held him for a long time, with her hands over his ears, afraid that something harsh might come to bring fear.

They sat there, in the straw.

It was done.

She held him in the patch of sunlight, trying to warm him with its spangles. She looked into his face.

For the first time, ever, in the whole of his life, the questions were gone.

She would never have to answer him again.

The doctors told Iris that it would be better if she did not plan to visit the mental hospital. They said

Hooker would not know her, and so she agreed not to go, because she knew she could not bear not to be known to him. It was best that she thought of him dead.

Later, when it had still not rained but time had had a chance to move, Iris walked out to Hooker's field and stood at its verge, in the trees.

She looked across the grass at the birds gathered on the far side, while they flew up, lightly, at the motion of her arrival. Then, no longer afraid, they settled back on their branches, staring.

Iris pursed her lips. A breeze rose somewhere near her shins. She felt cooled and quiet. Her black dress was mottled with green and yellow shade.

She stared. At her feet, Clementine's grave, the squirrel's grave, the graves of mice and birds and toads and frogs spread around her, dry, dusty, and welded with grass. There was just one grave, one silence.

Iris shaded her eyes and took her final look at the field.

"Oh, Lord," she thought. "This is such a dreadful feeling, thinking things have got to have an end."

She bowed her head with an impotent wish for prayer.

In the sky there was the noise of birds.

The changing of the season had come at last.

Faraway, a dog barked, and further still, a faint human voice, calling the dog's comforting, ordinary name, baffled the wilderness where she stood.

Iris stared.

Over the first low crest of the hill, from farther

north, and journeying, the flights of geese came, high
and pointed.

She began to hum, and then, to sing:

> "Frankie and Johnnie were lovers!
> Oh, lordy, how they could love...."

She sang the tune as she had in the old days, liking
the words and loving the song.

Above her, the birds had reconnoitered the field,
but flew straight on. Perhaps it was because their journey was so long before them. Perhaps it was because
the place below them was so suddenly alive with her
singing, and its grass was so hugely awash with the
movement of her slow, dark figure, clad in the motion
of its coat in the wind as she walked through the field
in the direction of a journey of her own.

Whatever their reason, it no longer mattered that
they did not pause. Next year, or another, they would
return.

The field and its welcome would always be there.

TIMOTHY FINDLEY

STONES

Against a vivid terrain of images, Findley continues his exploration of the many diverse and destructive acts played out on the personal battlegrounds on which we live our daily lives.

From the realities of contemporary relationships to a fantastic vision of urban life; from social comment to the deeply personal — *Stones* is a powerful collection of stories from one of Canada's best-loved writers.

A PENGUIN BOOK

"Findley is one of the world's greatest storytellers, and in
The Telling of Lies he has a marvellous tale to tell."
— *The Globe and Mail*

TIMOTHY FINDLEY

the telling of lies

THE BODY
is that of Calder Maddox, who owned half the world
and rented the other half.

THE SLEUTH
is Nessa Van Horne, whose photos of the beach on the
day of the murder may obscure more than they reveal.

THE SUSPECTS
are the many people who spend their summers at the
beautiful Aurora Sands Hotel. Could it be Lily, Calder's
diaphanous mistress? Or Nigel, the perfect civil servant?
Or the disappearing chauffeur? Or the mysterious doctor who
appears from nowhere?

A PENGUIN BOOK

TIMOTHY FINDLEY

Not Wanted on the Voyage

"It is one of those rare books that provide delight and
surprise and sometimes a shock on every page."
— *The Montreal Gazette*

Not Wanted on the Voyage is the story of the great flood and the
first time the world ended. It is a brilliant, unforgettable drama
filled with an extraordinary cast of characters: the tyrannical
Noah and his indomitable wife, Mrs. Noyes; the aging and
irritable Yaweh; Lucy (the enigmatic, disturbing woman who is
not what she seems); Mottyl (Mrs. Noyes's endearing talking cat);
a chorus of singing sheep and a unicorn destined for a horrible
death. With pathos and pageantry, desperation and hope, magic
and mythology, *Not Wanted on the Voyage* weaves
its unforgettable spell.

A PENGUIN BOOK

TIMOTHY FINDLEY

the WARS

WHAT HE DID WAS TERRIBLE AND BRAVE...

Robert Ross, a sensitive nineteen year old Canadian officer went
to war — The War to End All Wars. He found himself in the
nightmare world of trench warfare; of mud and smoke; of
chlorine gas and rotting corpses. In this world gone mad, Robert
Ross performed a last desperate act to declare his commitment to
life in the midst of death.

"He did the thing that no one else would even
dare to think of doing."

WAS IT AN ACT OF COMPASSION
OR AN ACT OF MADNESS?

"*The Wars* is quite simply one of the best novels
of the Great War... A magnificent book."
— *Vancouver Province*

 A PENGUIN BOOK

TIMOTHY FINDLEY

famous last words

"It is one of those rare books that provide delight and
surprise and sometimes a shock on every page."
— *The Montreal Gazette*

In the final days of the Second World War, Hugh Selwyn
Mauberley scrawls his desperate account on the walls and
ceilings of his ice-cold prison high in the Austrian Alps.
Officers of the liberating army discover his frozen, disfigured
corpse and his astonishing testament — the sordid truth that
he alone possessed. Fascinated but horrified, they learn of a
dazzling array of characters caught up in scandal and political
corruption. The exiled Duke and Duchess of Windsor, von
Ribbentrop, Hitler, Charles Lindbergh, Sir Harry Oakes —
all play sinister parts in an elaborate scheme to secure
world domination.

In a brilliant blending of fiction and historical fact, *Famous Last
Words* in another highly acclaimed novel by the award-winning
author of *The Wars, Not Wanted On the Voyage* and
The Telling of Lies.

●

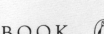

A PENGUIN BOOK

no longer.

He stood up, waved aside the shadows, and moved across the room. A soft, invisible, dry sweat-scented dream of dragonflies flew in a dusty cloud around him. Clittering with insinuating whispers, they flew inside his ears. He reached the window. He motioned with his hands. He tried to push away the noise.

Little Bones watched him.

Hooker pulled on his running shoes and gym shorts, and lifted up the box that he had hidden in the curtains by the window. The wood it was made of was cool, and he paused to notice it against him.

His head pounded.

Closing his eyes at last, he envisaged his journey.

He would go from room to room.

He went to the door and opened it.

The hall was gray and silent, but in a moment Iris might walk along it, going to the kitchen to begin her ordinary day, and he did not want to see her.

He stood very still, clutching the box up to his chest.

He surveyed the row of doors, but his eyes were so hot they were almost blind.

He could go from room to room. No.

No. They would hear him, and they must not. He would go to the stable. Somehow, in the stable, they would have to come to him.

He went along, down the hall and down the long arch of the stairs, passing the sleepers one by one, while they, unaware of him, shifted in their beds and did not dream.

The stable doors made no noise as they closed.

Outside, a few sweet-voiced birds had flown down

into the yard and were trying the earth for insects and for worms. What noise they made was small and distant.

Now Hooker wore a blond straw hat with ribbons that dangled down over his shoulders.

Daylight was growing, even inside the stable, and it revealed Hooker as a tan-faced boy with lanky, red-brown hair and green eyes. He was small and smooth, and in motion exactly like a cat—quick, deft, and quiet He toed in when he walked, and his arms hung down, bent a little at the elbow and again at the wrist, so that he could use his hands at once, very quickly, for whatever purpose he might find.

In the old stable where his grandfather's carriage and riding horses had once been, he stood, listening and stilled, in the center of the concrete floor. A large black-and-brown stain gave off the dried-up smell of axle grease and oil.

There was the smell, too, of old green straw and a bitter smell from oily cobwebs and a smell of rusted, dampish metal that came from the bars and fixtures of the horse stalls down one side. Each stall had an old banged gate of its own, and each was long emptied of horses or even the smell of them. It was lonely in the stable, and always empty now.

Hooker climbed up into the loft, where the bale door was half open, and he could look out through the sun-and-dust streamers to the back of the house. He lay down there and tried to flatten away the continuing sense of dizziness that circled around inside him. He set the box down, shifted it until it was level with his eyes, and then ignored it.